ARTEMISIA

Artemisia

OR

THE

PASSION

OF

PAINTING

MARINE BRAMLY
TRANSLATED BY C. DICKSON

WELCOME RAIN
NEW YORK

ARTEMISIA *by Marine Bramly.*

Originally published in France as Artemisia ou la passion de peindre.

Copyright © 1997 Editions Jean-Claude Lattès.

Translation © 2000 Welcome Rain Publishers LLC.

All right reserved.

Printed in the United States of America.

Direct any inquiries to Welcome Rain Publishers LLC, 532 Laguardia Place, Box 473, New York, NY 10012.

ISBN 1–56649–047–2

Manufactured in the United States of America by BLAZE I.P.I.

BOOK DESIGN BY JENNY DOSSIN

First Edition: January 2000

1   3   5   7   9   10   8   6   4   2

ARTEMISIA

I

Here I am, leaning over his face. My knees are firmly squeezing his hips. My buttocks are pressing against his abdomen. It's a difficult position to hold. With my left hand sinking into the mattress, the right one holds the carved ivory handle of the paintbrush.

I am Judith resuscitating Holofernes.

The Jewish merchant woman hadn't deceived me; her unguent marvelously masks the ugly blotches on the skin. Applying the concoction, I believe I can identify it as a mixture of fat, white lead, and cheap perfume.

The layer adheres well to the wan face. I still need to add the colors, rectify the curve of the eyebrow, the flaccid contours of the mouth. Time is running short, I work rapidly, heaving small sighs of disgust mingled with affection.

Next to the dead man's head, my cosmetic case lies open: the pink that normally serves to freshen my cheeks will add a bit of color to his, the gray and the green that lend mystery to my eyes will bring some expression back into his, the red that emphasizes the sensuality of my lips will bring life back to this cold mouth. Visitors will begin coming at dawn, strings of friends, of courtiers, investors, and mourners.

To them, he will appear to be sleeping.

Around his balding crown, whose sparse white hairs I have carefully painted, the rows of candles are like a halo. Was this man a saint or a tyrant? This is no time for passing judgment.

Draughts of air cause the candlelight to grow suddenly brighter, or to dim. The heat given off enhances the odor of putrefaction, sweet mustiness mixed with the smell of tallow. I am seized with a terrible fit of silent laughter: never have I had a more docile model. I, whose profession it is to transform living beings into mirages that I coax out of canvas, today find myself straddling an inert subject, made of flesh and bones, who I'm striving to reanimate.

The face gradually takes on life. I paint in the emotions that the dead man never allowed himself to show during his lifetime. My fingers lift the corners of his mouth before rigor mortis stiffens them for eternity. Two shadows slowly fade: I give him the smile of the divine Leonardo's Mona Lisa; it looks perfect on his face.

The light of dawn is now paling that of the candles. I can already hear the muffled voices out in the vestibule, footsteps coming up the stairs. So I lay down the paintbrush, quickly spread out the make-up base with my thumb to cover the large flat surfaces. I stand up one last time over the ice-cold body and step back to better assess my work.

A perfect illusion: Orazio Gentileschi, my father, looks more than ever like himself.

With the aid of his assistant, the undertaker lowers the casket into the hole. Several fresh graves on either side: the fall air is treacherous. Death is a familiar face in London at this time of year. I wasn't able to locate a Catholic priest. Little matter, we all pray to the same god.

Trembling in the cold damp breeze, the pastor recites the funeral oration; Latin suffused with an English accent. Someone blows into a handkerchief, another person coughs, and my fellow countrymen joke quietly in Roman dialect. Except for them, the whole cortège seems like a somber, faceless stream to me. I stare at the long oaken case. Did I make the right choice? A dense wood was obviously called for, to counter the lightness of his tired old body, but now I find the hastily varnished green boards a bit shocking. I would have preferred a darker patina, a few cracks to symbolize the age and the experience of the deceased would

4

have been more respectful. Why do I always entertain such petty thoughts at the most painful moments? Undoubtedly to keep suffering at bay, using the most conventional of weapons, banality, as a shield. All the while, horrid images are assailing me, vying for precedence in my mind: I can't keep from imagining Papa in his last resting place, being submitted day in and day out to the ravages of time, his rotting flesh devoured by legions of fastidious worms.

This morning I scraped the thick, crackled paint from his painter's palette, the same palette that's been with him since he was in Rome, then I crushed the multicolored flakes into a fine powder with a mortar and pestle.

My hand is preparing to pay the last homage; all of my thoughts are centered on this small heap of dust in which grains of vermilion and sky blue can still be detected. Yes, paint rather than soil, it seems much more appropriate to me.

The handful of mixed pigments rains slowly down upon the coffin.

"Artemisia," a voice cries out. "Artemisia!"

Who can be calling to me that way? I stop listening. Can't they leave me in peace? It's all over with, I'm going now.

Every time that a chapter in my life closes, a host of memories comes flooding back to me in tight little waves. The vague impressions, the blurry reminiscences change into a clear vision in which events are almost arranged in chronological order.

Oddly enough, it is aboard the ship that is carrying me back to Italy that I suddenly feel I understand the full impact of the many months I have just spent in London.

Why had I traveled there, at almost fifty years of age, when I had more than enough work and my life in Italy couldn't have been better?

I remember my brother Marco, bursting into my studio in Florence unannounced. My only link with the past, he and I had never lost contact. My mother died when I was a child, and I hadn't seen my father in years.

Marco had been sent to deliver an invitation from King Charles I: I was called upon to join Orazio in the English court, which was anxious to be honored by my presence.

My younger brother spoke at length about the state of our father's health, his strength was dwindling. It had gotten to the point that one questioned his ability to complete the ceilings for the queen's palace in Greenwich, for which my father had already received and exhausted his advance.

I was morally bound by the contract. In a way, painters of the same family inherit debts. Although the royal invitation was formulated in polite, even flattering terms, mentioning a *Tarquin and Lucretia* of my own hand, purportedly the centerpiece of Her Majesty's collection, the unequivocal order underlying the compliments came through very clearly.

King Charles, whose main obsession was luring Italian artists to his court, and whose numerous offers I had declined until now, undoubtedly believed he had found an irrefutable argument this time.

He was mistaken, at least about one point; my profession had made a rich woman of me, financial problems were the least of my worries, and I could have easily settled my father's accounts. But by some strange fluke of love, suddenly what was most important to me was my father's honor. Once Papa was gone, or too weakened with age, the great frescoes he had begun would be entrusted to some nameless drudge or other. The responsibility for completing them would fall to that scheming Trattore, to the incompetent Staggiano, who had already immigrated to London, or even worse, to one of those lame Englishmen who, try as they might to imitate the Italian manner of painting, never come close. No other paintbrush would besmirch the last work of Orazio Gentileschi; it had become a matter of principle to me.

So it was that I departed immediately for the northern mists, abandoning my own work and—to be honest—happy to be putting an end to a feud that had lasted over thirty years.

Orazio wasn't expecting me so soon, or perhaps not at all. Still in my traveling apparel, I stood there observing him in silence, hidden by the scaffolding. He was sitting under the high ceilings of Queen's House, in the middle of a vast and cluttered room. Where had his assistants gone? Where was all the usual racket of the work site? Why this deathly calm? Had Orazio sent his aids away so that he could be alone? He stretched his arms out in front of himself like a blind man, his hands were trembling.

I didn't dare come out from my hiding place. He had cut short his gesture with a kind of rage and remained prostrate, at a loss, his head sunk between his knees.I didn't feel I had the right to be witnessing this scene. If I had come forward then, my father would have died of shame. So I waited quietly for the right moment.

An eternity passed before Orazio finally got to his feet and began to regain some of his old pride, his dignified stance, his determined look. It was like a resurrection, a transfiguration. My father always did want everything to look like a painting.

Light and shadow suddenly seemed to intermingle and restore calm to his emaciated features, imbue them with force, allow an aura of glory to emanate from him.

I then ventured forth to meet him. The high vaulted ceilings reverberated with my echoing footsteps. He didn't recognize me at first—I must have changed quite a bit myself since we last had seen each other. A muffled cry escaped my lips, "Papa!" I felt as though I were pronouncing that word for the very first time—a call coming from the very depths of my being, filling me with warmth.

His eyes lit up. He opened his arms and I ran to them.

Our partnership lasted for one year, until that fated February 7, in 1639, the day of his death.

Side by side, my father and I worked in perfect harmony on the ceiling of the grand hall. We never again mentioned the past, or all of the painful things that had separated us—the reproaches, the scandalous trial. The king had ordered a fresco exalting the prosperity of his reign; we had proposed an allegory representing Peace and the Arts flourishing under the crown of England for the central lunette. The image of this fecund Peace is the central figure in the composition. As if in silent agreement, the allegory symbolized first and foremost the peace that we had reestablished between ourselves, and it was a much more successful pact than if it had been clenched with words, more enduring than if it had been inscribed in ink, in Latin before a notary: it was an immense pictorial reconciliation that mankind would admire under the royal dome for centuries to come.

Side by side, without speaking, totally absorbed in our task for days on end, we strove with all our souls to accomplish this common work. I no longer held any resentment. As for him, he never asked me why I had abandoned him for so long.

As the work progressed and developed, so did our own peace of mind. Deep within ourselves, by means of the fresco that had brought us together, our story was being secretly rewritten. Strengthened by the wisdom that comes with age, with lassitude, and with hindsight, I forgave him for all the pain he had caused me. It seemed as if our love had never been spoiled by any discord. And, since I was beginning to realize that it had also emancipated me from his all-powerful influence as my father, even the nightmare he had made me live through simply changed into an ordinary memory.

Now, we were on such an equal basis that we formed but one being. What mysterious alchemy comes into play with painting! While one of us applied the large flat surfaces of shadow, the other placed the touches of light; my father would sketch the mouth of a muse, I would draw in the nose, the eyebrows; we would correct one another, perfect one another; he would roughly shape part of a body and I would brush in the rest, and the two parts melded together seamlessly, meshed without leaving the slightest trace of duality.

That period was a truce, a miraculous remission. Under the royal ceilings my father seemed to have taken on new force, as if he fed on my own energy. And yet nights, in my room that was next to his, I could hear the deathly cough that racked his chest.

I would have liked to be able to breathe my vital fluids into him just as he had once transmitted the science of his art to me.

And so, as if to flee the presence of death, whose inexorable progression I could feel through the bedroom wall, I would slip away, escape onto the wayward paths of memory, allowing myself to cast off this envelope of a mature woman each night in order to become once again, at the side of the Orazio I recalled, the young Artemisia of times past.

2

Tuzia, my stepmother, had pulled a brilliant maneuver. I spent my fifteenth birthday in the convent like a respectable young lady. What is Tuzia so afraid of? Of the affection that my father bears for me? She really needn't worry, Orazio's heart is big enough for all of us. And anyway, Papa isn't her personal trophy.

It's true, from the time I got out of diapers, my whole life has been spent in the studio, and it's not exactly the ideal place for properly raising a girl, but there's nothing I can do about that. It's something that was beyond my control.

When I'm in the studio, I feel as though I'm in my natural element. All of the props strewn about, accessories everywhere, scattered pots of pigment, mysterious vials, dusty scrolls, not to mention the mirrors fitted with candles and the oilcloth screens: it's all part of my essential makeup.

I grew up surrounded by all of that. Colors, lights, all sorts of matter to fascinate me. I'm in heaven with the coarse conversation and the pungent sweat of the assistants nearby.

I did everything imaginable to be allowed to remain in the studio. Slipping under the easels, I would constantly repeat to Papa, "I might be small, but I can be very useful." I did my best to anticipate his slightest need, so he would not banish me. One moment I would be completely unobtrusive and the next I'd be acting the fool. I modeled for any and all subjects. At the snap of his fingers, I would drape myself in the robes of angels, shepherds, infantes, or pages. I could hold a pose better than anyone. I scorned the use of the thin cords that, looped around one's wrists or ankles, could so alleviate sore members in difficult poses. Tensing my muscles and clenching my teeth, without it ever showing, I could stand for hours on end just to please my father.

My stepmother would have preferred me to drudge about in the kitchen, or help her with the laundry and the housework. She would always say to me, "You aren't Orazio's son, Artemisia, you're his daughter!"

Today, I would answer her, "You should have swept up the studio more carefully, Tuzia. The bits of chalk lying about on the floor look so untidy, and they're very tempting for young children."

I was no exception to the rule, and I furiously set about marking on the floors, the outside walls, the smallest scrap of paper that fell into my hands. At first, when you saw my scribbling, Tuzia, you threatened to call my father so he would beat me, then you came closer and looked longer at my drawings; you didn't say another word. Kneeling down, using the hem of your skirt to erase them, you glared at me as though I had uttered some sort of blasphemy. You made me swear I would never do it again.

I was seven years old. My mother had just died in bringing my brother, Marco, into the world. The house was unkempt, our young housemaid's cooking wasn't fit to eat, and Marco and I were neglected, left to our own devices. As a loyal neighbor, who had been recently widowed, you offered to lend a hand. Very rapidly, as if our two houses were not close enough, you decided to move in with us. Mama's funeral was barely over with when you began sharing my father's bed. Maybe you had shared it beforehand, who knows?

Good fortune had rid you of the wife. As for the daughter, you were determined to find a solution.

Papa ended up taking you as his second wife. You got your brand new dress, your noisy celebration, you reveled in the newfound respect that you now inspired. "Signora Gentileschi": the title made you strut about proudly for months. You could have just cooed with pleasure.

Then that no longer satisfied you, you wanted to isolate Papa from the rest of the world. I must admit that his slightly misanthropic penchant was a big help to you.

We piled all of our possessions onto two carts and went into exile, leaving Rome behind us, along with all the stimulating activity of the via della Croce and the artists' quarter. You had insisted on only one thing—leaving Rome. You could not have cared less about the destination.

My father Orazio managed to dig up the ideal place for our retreat, a calm little village, lost in an immensity of lush vegetation, approximately thirty leagues from the capital. A single street snaked between the drystone houses that stood baking in the sun, and yet remained cool inside. Our back door opened on to the pine forest and the dunes.

The sea wasn't visible, but the crashing sound of the waves was barely muted, the smell of salt filled the air, the cries of seagulls were everywhere. In the evenings, on their way back from the beach, the fishermen sang songs in a gay dialect that I quickly learned. I was delighted with this new life. I gallivanted about with tousled hair, sunburnt cheeks and skinned knees, utterly carefree.

And then there was Fulvio, a fisherman's son, my friend. With his blond curls, his delicate face, his blue eyes, and his deerlike gait, Fulvio looked so much like a legendary young prince that I always expected his rags to turn into a brocaded doublet. I would help him mend his nets and tell him tales of the big city; he taught me all about the sea and, with a pin, extracted the spines of sea urchins, embedded painfully in my feet.

We played make-believe and pretended we were wed in the little chapel by the sea.

The day that a drop of blood spread out to make a red cloud in the water of the basin, my whole life changed. Tuzia told my father that I had become a woman and that I must now stay at home. No more dunes, no more Fulvio. Tuzia knew that Orazio didn't want to be separated from me, so she calculated her move to be carried out in two phases—first reclusion, then eviction.

The young assistants in the studio had always treated me with respect. Tuzia took to making insidious little comments in front of them. As soon as my father's back was turned, she would publicly evoke the transformations my body was going through. I didn't realize what she was up to. I had been brought up surrounded by bodies, in adoration of bodies. Rather than covering myself modestly, I laughed. Sandro and Pietro, two apprentices who were barely older than I, joined in my laughter. They cracked blatantly vulgar jokes; I kept on laughing.

One day my father overheard them and had them beaten and then dismissed. Not knowing which way to turn, he was at a complete loss. How could he continue to protect my virtue in an environment filled with men? Tuzia came up with a marvelous solution, the convent.

3

It was a huge reddish building with a tiled roof, two days drive from our village, half church and half prison. The high walls surrounded a square garden in which medicinal herbs were planted. Lilies, the symbol of purity, were the only flowers that grew in the shadow of its steeple.

That edifice terrified me at first sight. I never completely got over the feeling of fear it inspired in me. Admittedly, the stories that went around the place, and that had been passed down from one generation of inmates to the next, were enough to give one gooseflesh.

Rumor had it that a *condottiero* founded the convent in the beginning of the sixteenth century and, as a form of repentance, would lock up the farm girls he had ravished there. As soon as they became pregnant, he would force them to dedicate their lives to God and would arrange for the fruits of their sins to conveniently disappear. It was also whispered that several years ago, when work was undertaken in the cellars of the west wing, the workmen had unearthed dozens of tiny fetal and newborn skeletons.

The other girls in the convent claim that this tradition was never abandoned. According to them, we sleep on a cemetery filled with bastard children.

I was told that we virgins never run into the poor sinners. They come to the convent from all over the country when they have just learned of their pregnancy, to allegedly take a short retreat from the world. Violetta, a scrawny young girl who puts horsehair between her skin and her clothing as an act of contrition, says that their quarters are separate from ours. Their little problem is taken care of, and one fine day they leave for home with a flat stomach, while new corpses regenerate the earth under the convent. I don't really believe all of that, but it doesn't keep me from despising this place.

For the past hour we've been alternately kneeling down and then rising. Every time the priest motions us to rise, I get to my feet as quickly as possible, the blood rushes to my head, I see stars. It's very powerful, and it feels good.

Sister Mary is keeping an eye on me. She immediately noticed that I don't sing along with the other girls. Liturgical music is so beautiful, it fills my soul with delight, it even makes faint shudders run down my spine. But I just can't manage to remember all those complicated words, and besides, I always sing off-key. So I end up just moving my lips. Since I can't hear the sound of my own voice, and my lips are moving, I feel as though all of that music is coming from my throat exactly as if I had a hundred voices.

We spend an amazing amount of time in the chapel. I don't mind it though, there are some beautiful frescoes here.

Above all, there's a Descent from the Cross, in which the suffering is admirably depicted, it obviously drives the other girls to hysterics. With the exception of the old priest in his burlap robe and the pimple-ridden choir boy, men are rare around here and Jesus is a man, after all. If one ignores the subject, all that remains is the thin muscular body, languishing and on the verge of death, cradled in a woman's arms. Do the girls in the convent secretly imagine themselves in the place of the Virgin Mary?

I too, see other things: the perfectly mixed glaze, the originality of the line, the harmonious rendition of flesh tones. As far as the pose goes, its classical rigidity is not to my taste.

A nun casts an angry look at me, motions to me with her chin to keep my eyes on the altar.

I docilely bow my head. I'm quite pious in my own way, but I just can't help it, I'm easily distracted. The nice thing about mass is that the choreography is so repetitive. Once you catch on to the rhythm, you can be a thousand leagues away, and still not miss a single step.

The priest pronounces the final words, *Ite missa est,* and starts down the central aisle as we are leaving our pews. Taking advantage of the relative confusion, I pluck one of the candles from the spiked holder. A short thick candle, made to last. My fingertips moistened with saliva snuff out the flame. I quickly conceal my theft under my blouse.

No one saw me. A drop of hot wax trickles down to cool on my breast. I think of the story of the young Spartan who hid a fox cub under his tunic. Rather than admit his crime, he had unblinkingly allowed the animal to eat away at his stomach. What would I do if the mother superior ever— My thoughts are abruptly cut off, we are already forming a nice orderly line, a veritable string of cherubs in nun's garb.

Many of the girls in the convent have faces that seem to be polished and uplifted, rubbed smooth with spirituality. Mine is contorted with apprehension, and excitement too. I hope it doesn't show. I would be condemned to solitary confinement in the hole for a crime like this. The girls say that in the hole, the phantoms of tortured babies come to suckle at one's breasts at night. Poor little immolated children, whether you be real or imagined, may the earth lie lightly upon your frail bones!

Each in turn, we genuflect in the direction of the altar, and I whisper one last prayer to God, "Please let the time pass quickly, I'm eager to return to my cell."

This day seems to drag on endlessly. Despite the fact that the candle is soft and smooth, it rubs so against my naked flesh that it feels as though there are hot coals under my blouse.

The midday meal, prayers, a lesson in spinning, prayers, catechism, training in household duties, prayers, a lesson in gardening. I feign a sudden backache to avoid the hoeing and weeding. Bending over in that way, the candle would surely have fallen out.

As dinner draws on, I caress the stem of wax through my clothing. I love this candle with a passion. It isn't the first one, and it won't be the last to open the doors of learning to me. I steal one every week. They never last more that one night, and I spend the six other nights of the week waiting eagerly for the next candle. I don't dare pilfer them more often. The nun in charge of supplies would end up noticing. We are not allowed to have any light in our cells. Night is intended for sleeping. The sisters say it's a matter of humility, of piety: we are insignificant creatures in the hands of God, no other light should guide us but that of the Most High. In reality, I suspect them of skimping in the name of tightfisted economic measures.

The little bell rings. Finally!

Silently, lightly, we ascend the worn steps leading to our quarters, like a flight of young swallows. Walk in a straight line, veer off to the side when one's cell is reached.

Ten stone arches skillfully ventilate the corridor that leads out to the cloister's garden. At the very end, just before reaching my room, a large arch frames a wide open landscape—a gentle slope planted with orange trees, laurels, and vineyards rustling with the coming night. It's like a painting. I sometimes feel like vaulting over the parapet and running off into the canvas just to wander about for a while. But not today.

I hurry into my room, I call it "my cubicle." It is four steps wide and five steps long and contains a hard, narrow cot. No table and no chair. A pitcher, a mug, and a chamber pot.

Hanging on the wall, a Virgin Mary seems to be gazing beyond the cramped quarters of the cell. Only religious images are allowed within the precincts of the convent. And even so, only one per cell. Young Rosa, the girl who cries at night, hung up several images the day she arrived. The mother superior had immediately ordered her to take them off the walls.

"Sinful vanity, my child! Pious images are not intended for *decorating* the cells of God's servants."

My Virgin is the guardian of my soul but also of the treasures that I hide behind the canvas, tucked safely under the wooden frame. I smuggled them in. Lord forgive this sinner! Among these treasures is a little mirror that used to belong to my mother.

How long has it been since I last glimpsed the reflection of my face, undistorted by the unevenness of a windowpane or the ripples in water? Religion forbids mirrors, we are not to look at anything but our hands. We accomplish our weekly ablutions fully dressed, in the half-light, scrubbing the flesh under our robes with a blind cloth. Don't the sisters know that fingers can sometimes see more clearly than eyes?

Tonight I undress quickly, keeping on only my long cotton chemise. I'll leave my door ajar until Sister Ennemonda completes her evening rounds; that's the rule.

I hide the candle under the mattress and slip down between the sheets.

The sister soon appears, a spectral image with a winged cornet. She comes silently over to the bed, plunges her rough palms under the quilt, grabs hold of my hands, the horrid touch, and brings them out from beneath the bedclothes to lay them prudently on either side of my body. She tucks the covers in tightly. Who does she think she's fooling? Does she really believe I'll fall for her little trick? That it will keep me from putting my arms back under the sheets? Keep me from sticking my fingers still deeper into the intimate folds of my flesh if I feel like it?

I listen closely to the sound of her fading footsteps, like a little mouse trotting away, bloated with mute self-righteousness.

The quilt is rapidly tossed aside. Groping through darkness, I reach the corridor where a tiny pilot light trembles. I dip the wick of my candle into the flame, protecting it from the onslaughts of wind, and run back to my cell as quickly as my legs will carry me.

Before I can take down the Virgin Mary, I still need to block the latchless door with my iron cot.

The very first time, in the wavering light of the candle, I had timidly stretched out my hand toward the mirror that lay shiny and new upon the bed. It is so small that at first I could only see the triangle formed by my eyes, nose, and mouth. The oval shape of my cheeks, my hair, and my ears, as well as my neck, were not reflected in the small glass.

My eyes were still clear and seemed more determined than before, as though they were now filled with a driving purpose. The bridge of my nose was more pronounced, narrower too. I discovered that my lips were fuller than they had been when I was a child. From the little I was able to make out in the tiny mirror, I was prompted to stammer, "I think I've grown to be quite pretty." Then I stuck my tongue out at myself.

Slowly the mirror pivoted in my hands, revealing the roundness of my cheekbones, the dark sheen of my curls, and I had believed I was still a blonde. I murmured to myself, "One day you'll become a great painter, Artemisia."

Not a sound to be heard. I take off my nightgown as though I were casting off a heavy cloak. I'm eager to start to work.

Now I am naked, sitting cross-legged on the bed surrounded by all of my treasures: sheets of paper, red clay crayons. The mattress cover is thin, the horse hairs are sticking through it and tickling the backs of my thighs; I don't find it displeasing. In my right hand I'm holding the bit of crayon fitted into a reed holder; in the left, the mirror. I raise myself onto my knees, twist around to make the muscles stand out, so that I can better see them.

Feverishly, I transcribe onto the paper the snatches of body that spring to life in the mirror. Shading the sanguine color with my middle finger to bring out the contrasts, I can hear my father's voice in my mind, repeating to his assistants, "The shadows of an object itself are always lighter than the shadow it casts."

First I draw a foot. It is of classical Greek proportions. Then the slightly thick ankle, the bulge of the calf near the knee, the cone-shaped thigh, rather plump where it is joined to the buttocks.

Afterward, the abdomen, a swell of soft flesh.

Next the breasts, iridescent pulp streaked with veins.

The shape of the arms resembles that of the legs.

Finally, my overly long, slightly old-fashioned hands.

The pubis simply appears as an etched-in shadow. I'm still not daring enough to spread my legs and actually study it.

For a long time, I simply drew from memory. I got in the habit of using my eyes like a crayon. I would follow the outlines of everything I came upon. The apple on the breakfast table, the other girls in prayer, the barnyard animals. . . . Then closing my eyelids, I would transcribe what I'd just seen onto the screen they formed. As soon as I was able to find some paper, crayons and a candle; I began bringing everything I'd memorized back to my room and re-creating it on paper. Later, the mirror improved upon this ordinary bill of fare—I finally had a live model.

Nevertheless, I'm beginning to grow tired of myself. I'll have to persuade young Rosa to pose for me. She often cries at night, she obviously feels terribly lonely. I can tell that beneath her jumper, she has a body full of resources, both nicely rounded and well built. She'll undoubtedly be horror-stricken and refuse. It is forbidden for women to study from the nude; a woman who practices drawing is an evil creature, an instrument of the devil. Rosa just might go and reveal my secret. No one must know!

The fragments of my body come together on the paper to form entire bodies, strange women that seem to have been caught unexpectedly in moments of the utmost privacy. One of them seems to be waiting for something or for someone, another appears to be daydreaming, and still another, resisting some kind of temptation.

I'm intimidated by these women. And yet they are all me . . .

On other sheets of paper, I sketch out details: the curve of a shoulder, a languid hand, a neat row of toes.

The moon has already crossed the frame of my small window and disappeared. Ten or so drawings are scattered about on the floor at the foot of my bed.

I don't see the candle come unstuck from the lump of wax at its base, roll over the bedclothes, set fire to the sheets of paper and mattress. Or rather, I do see it, but it's already too late. There is smoke everywhere, I'm coughing and crying, helpless against the yellow and red flames.

In solitary confinement, I quickly lose all track of time. Sleep, gnaw on the dry crust of bread before some mouse makes off with it, sleep, don't let the water in the jug go stale, sleep, forget about the whip lashes stinging the flesh on my back, sleep, sleep to drive away the fear.

The door doesn't squeak; I always thought that the doors to these kinds of black holes would squeak. Sister Ennemonda comes silently in. She hasn't brought my ration of bread with her this time, nor the pitcher of water that I'm usually entitled to. Why is she carrying that basin of steaming water, that comb, those undergarments, the clean jumper? Why don't they leave me alone?

She motions for me to get up from my straw pallet. Judging from the way she looks at me, I must be in a sorry state. She has to wash me herself, I haven't got the strength. It's a strange feeling to be touched by those hands, devoid of all affection. I can sense that she is repulsed by me and yet she is also aroused.

Now Sister Ennemonda is leading me along by the arm. "The mother superior wishes to see you."

It is not daybreak yet. Dawn casts faint tinge of pink across the sky.

At first I don't understand where she is taking me; this isn't the way to the mother superior's quarters. We turn to the left, off of the main covered walk, cross the antechambers. Then I realize that we are going to the reception room.

Why the reception room?

Who is that man with his back turned, looking out the windows?

My father doesn't greet me, he doesn't even look at me. He knows that I've committed a very serious offense. They wouldn't have sent for him otherwise. There are dark circles under his eyes; he's probably been traveling all night, his boots are white with dust.

I stand there with my head bowed. A desperate prayer is knocking about in my skull like a trapped bird. "Lord have pity upon me, would that my drawings were all burned! Please, Lord, let there be nothing left of them!

The Lord must be occupied elsewhere, or else he holds a terrible grudge against me. The mother superior shakes a small bell; Sister Ennemonda appears, with her mouth like a saber slash and carrying a pile of papers in her arms.

They have scarcely been damaged.

Orazio looks them over carefully. Anatomical studies, fine lines for the light areas, bold ones to render shadow. Sensually toned down with the thumb. He furrows his brow sternly.

Tuzia had warned me: "Your father will kill you if he learns that you practice drawing." My stepmother had made me promise never to draw again; I had never stopped; I should have obeyed her.

Papa lingers a little longer over one of the nudes. The mother superior vehemently pulls at my hair. "It will take you a century of penance to make up for this! You should be hanging your head in shame!"

Orazio slowly lifts his eyes from the paper. He contemplates me and, instead of the anticipated storm of deprecation, says, "There's no doubt about it, she's definitely the daughter of a painter."

I can't have understood correctly, it's not possible. I must still be in the hole, stuck in one of my dreams. . . . But no, my father's eyes are shining with pride.

Uncontrollable rage shakes the mother superior. "I must warn you," she hisses, "that laxness in the face of your daughter's impudence could compromise future orders from the churches in our diocese!"

My father shakes his head; he appears to feel truly sorry for her. "The orders are issued from the cardinal, Mother, and I doubt that His Eminence would allow his esthetic judgment to be influenced by a woman. . . . Even one as saintly as yourself."

And he stretches out his hand to me like God touching Adam at the dawn of humanity. A joyful smile breaks out on my face, and I believe that one is spreading on his as well.

"Come along, Misia," he says. "You still have a lot to learn."

Hugging me to his side, he adds, for the benefit of the mother superior, "But not here."

Papa's hand is still holding mine. It's the same viselike grip I knew as a child, that unconscious habit he has of squeezing my fingers so hard it almost hurts. It feels so reassuring, no one can take me away from him now. I almost want to dance.

My father's even steps echo strangely over the grounds of the convent. Heavy, powerful, determined footsteps. A man's footsteps.

Twenty sleepy faces suddenly appear in the vaulted archways of the dormitory, twenty cotton-clad torsos straining in curiosity toward the cloister gardens that we are crossing. My fellow prisoners are observing my departure. Some look dumbfounded, others jealous, and still others seem sad. I give them all friendly little waves of farewell, but in truth I am so happy to be leaving them that I murmur to myself: "Good-bye to Regina, who smells of codfish! Good-bye to cross-eyed Fabia! Good-bye to Violante, the future nun . . . !"

For Rosa, who cries at night, and who is crying in broad daylight for the very first time, I have this gentle thought: "Be brave, my friend, try and commit some terrible blunder that will get you thrown out of here!"

Two nuns follow us carrying my wooden trunk with heavy, metal-reinforced corners; they are staggering under the weight. For the first one, Sister Gianna, a wretched little pest, I make a wish that she'll sprain her back. For the second, Sister Magdalena, whom I really have nothing against, I simply mutter, "Poor soul!"

We climb into the hired carriage. The doors slam shut with a tremendous bang of freedom. If I could, I'd whip the horses myself and be off.

4

My little brother Marco must have been anxiously awaiting our arrival; as we pull up, he nearly dashes under the carriage wheels in his excitement. He's grown quite a bit; he looks like a mischievous little angel. I give him a big hug.

On the other hand, there are no effusive greetings with Tuzia. My stepmother has changed. That once handsome face of a Roman matron now betrays the insidious nature of her soul. Little bitter wrinkles line her brow, gather at the corners of her eyes and mouth.

I had promised myself during the journey that I would never let the resentment I feel toward her show. Tuzia seems to have made the same resolution. She gives me a bleak smile; her teeth are beginning to go bad. For just an instant, she's caught completely off-guard when my father says, "Go and muster up an apprentice's outfit for Artemisia."

The house hasn't changed a bit.

It doesn't take me long to make a new enemy: Roberto, my father's senior assistant, a tall dark and lanky youth, who is always hostile and vindictive toward women. Everyone calls him "The Lover," but never to his face—he'd probably beat us if we did.

At first, I didn't understand how he had come by such an ill-suited nickname. I asked Fabio, who comes from the same village, and he told me the whole story. When Roberto was only thirteen or fourteen years old, he fell madly in love with a certain Tita. One day, Roberto had mustered all of his courage and asked her to meet him behind the church. He came up to her trembling all over, took the girl's hands, and proclaimed his love for her. Tita encouraged him to pour out everything in his heart, and even more. Then she burst out with a shrill laugh. That was the signal: gales of laughter rang out from all sides.

Tita had spread the news around to Roberto's friends that there was going to be a fine show. The gang of kids had come sneaking up to the church and hidden in order to surprise the poor boy and ridicule him. They never stopped making fun of him. After that, no one ever called Roberto anything but "The Lover." That's the main reason he left his village, too.

Ever since that day, Roberto has detested women.

He's a native of Sicily, which doesn't help matters. Over there, when a baby boy is born, the father lifts him up toward the sky and proclaims, "God bless him!" If it is a girl, he turns his head away and mutters, "She'll peel potatoes."

I feel sorry for Roberto, but I just have no respect for him. I often have to bear the brunt of his hatred for women.

Maybe that's what makes him seem like such an opportunist. Always under his master's feet, like a jealous dog. But a dog with ambitions. Roberto plays the part of the devoted disciple. Yet I would wager that he would like to see my father dead and buried, that he would even be prepared to knock him over the head, provided he could pump everything he knew out of the master beforehand.

Roberto is afraid that I'll overshadow him. He spends most of his time pushing me around, giving me all the dirty work to do—work that is physically too hard for me—in order to prove that I'm incompetent. Or else he gives me the jobs that there's nothing to learn from, to keep me from progressing. He hates the idea of a girl wanting to become a painter. When I walked into the studio for the first time dressed in my apprentice's turban, shirt, and trousers, Roberto scoffed, "Indeed! The famous paintress . . . ," as if it were the most ridiculous thing in the world.

I felt like hurling an insult from his native land at him: "Go eat your own dead, Roberto!"

The rope is rubbing the skin off my fingers. It winds around my forearm and cuts into the flesh. My whole body is straining against the weight; the pulley is squeaking. I can barely control the cable that keeps my brother Marco suspended in the air, twelve cubits off the floor. Poor little boy, he's doing his best to look angelic. The leather halter strapped under his stomach makes it difficult for him to breathe. He's wearing a seraphim's costume with broad wings and, miserable from both nausea and cramped limbs, he holds a crown of flowers and a long palm leaf in his outstretched arms. An apprentice adjusts the pose with the aid of the fine cords tied to Marco's wrists and ankles. My brother looks like a marionette.

"Pull the lad up higher. Can't you see he's not in the light?"

I pull even harder on the rope, hearing the order barked out by that fool Roberto.

I cast a quick glance at the canvas. My father is busily applying the colors, attempting to catch the golden, almost unearthly light given off by the chandelier.

Frustrated, Orazio shakes his head, "Roberto!" he bellows, "pull the candles up higher, it's plain that the lighting is all wrong."

It serves Roberto right. He shouldn't have told me to pull harder on the rope.

"Right away, Master," and he has the gall to add, "it's just that Artemisia is always getting in the way and making it difficult to maneuver."

The dirty rat bumps into me as he passes by. I stomp on his foot on purpose. "Oh, pardon me, Roberto!"

The living picture is bathed in celestial light, an eerie little island surrounded by the fevered agitation of the studio.

On the raised platform beneath my younger brother, kneeling before an organ, on a purple cushion edged in gold, a farm girl poses as Saint Cecilia, the patron saint of music. Her hair has been washed and combed, her face is made-up, she is draped a white satin robe embroidered with lilies that intensifies the freshness of her complexion.

She seems astonished at finding herself here, in this studio, and looking so pretty. My father calls her back to order, "Saint Cecilia, look at Marco!"

Marco can't take anymore, his lips are trembling, he chokes back a little sob. Orazio leaves his easel and tugs affectionately at the rope, "Come now, Marco, what have you done with your angel's smile? Just a little bit longer son, we're almost finished."

Luckily, we're interrupted by a visitor. It's Nicolo, Papa's agent. He's terribly pretentious. He's always dressed in the latest fashion. His sumptuous clothing speaks eloquently of the commissions my father pays him.

Nicolo has come to confirm a new order. Here goes, they'll be talking about finances again!

In the studio, Art is considered secondary to Gold. This has even become one of the principle topics of conversation in our home. Tuzia insists that father should limit himself to portraits and paint scores of them. She's always repeating, "At least with portraits, the models pay you." And she often adds, "Instead of it being you who remunerate them!"

I listen distractedly to what Nicolo is saying. "The canvas will measure forty square feet," he begins. "The background will be priced at two ecus per square foot."

"That makes eighty ecus for the background," Papa remarks impatiently.

"The Virgin Mary and the Archangel Gabriel. There will be only two figures," Nicolo continues. "I was able to obtain seven ecus for the man and three for the woman. Seven plus three, ten. Which brings the total fee to—"

Exasperated, I interrupt, "Why such a discrepancy in price? Isn't there just as much to paint in a woman as there is in a man? The same number of arms, legs, ears eyes—?"

"Silence," my father cuts me off, "if you own a pair of eyes, use them to look gratefully upon the ecus that land in our coffers."

I leave the studio clenching my fists as Roberto looks on mockingly.

Red-cheeked, I go off to my room to change my clothes. I take off the turban that protects my hair, step out of my paint-splattered trousers, unfasten my shirt. I've now developed the muscles of a boy, though I still feel somewhat sore due to the daily exercise. I play for a moment at flexing them under the skin. Then I pull on a dress and go tearing down the stairs.

It's not easy to have been born a woman in a man's world. My whole body is filled with rage. I need to cast off this anger the way a horse shakes its body to rid itself of bothersome insects.

So I go running out toward the dunes. When I reach their crest, I lay down sideways on the slope. Just the slightest impulse, and there I go, rolling down to the bottom. Sand gets in my mouth, seeps under my eyelids, as I roll faster and faster, so fast that it seems as if I'm not moving at all, while my body is buffeted with curious sensations. At the bottom of the slope, as I'm still rolling, I feel myself being lifted off the ground. I scream in fear, then burst out laughing.

"Gracious! You frightened me, Fulvio!"

I recognize my friend, the young fisherman. He sets me back down on my feet, smiling playfully. The sea air has sculpted his face, just as the waves sculpt rock. His features are not as even as they used to be, yet they are stronger, handsome and mysterious. He must be about seventeen years old now. Fulvio brandishes a necklace of live fish that are flopping around and pretends to try to slip it around my neck.

"For you, princess," he exclaims, "jewels from the sea!"

Even fresh fish can smell awfully strong. I push the bizarre necklace away, strangling back a laugh. "Pew! Take it away!"

He continues to play the fool, putting on a contrite, almost offended look. "But it has all the colors that you love," he objects, rinsing the fish in a pool of water to revive their colors. "Look—red, green, yellow, silver—just like in a painting!" Then he murmurs, "Do you remember the day that we were married in the little chapel by the sea?" There is a strange light in his eyes. Since I don't answer him, he stares fixedly at my chest and in a brusque, almost aggressive tone, his voice suddenly hoarse, blurts out, "So your breasts have grown, eh?"

I feel uneasy. Fulvio senses my embarrassment and starts clowning again. He purposefully dons an idiotic grin, swaggers grotesquely over to me, and feigns stealing a kiss.

It doesn't make me laugh. I turn and run away.

5

Cuddled up close to one another on the large pallet thrown down in a corner of the room, the young apprentices are lost in deep and determined sleep. A row of incomplete paintings leans up against the opposite wall. Some, barely dry, are astoundingly lifelike. Scattered here and there are a few stuffed animals, a cat, two turtle doves, a peacock, and even a horse's head. Piles of empty pigment pots, paintbrushes hanging from nails or soaking in jars. Strange utensils, implausible paraphernalia, stray props in every spare corner.

The studio seems very calm at this hour. I love to come here, nights, when I can't sleep: to sit down on the bare floor and let a feeling of listlessness creep over me, a feeling of buoyancy, punctuated with thoughts that are almost visions.

One of the children stirs restlessly in his sleep, disturbed by a nightmare. I carry the oil lamp over to the bedside; it's Vito. I stroke his hair to calm him. Poor child, he's twelve years old, only three years older than my brother Marco. He's been with my father for about six months now. He comes from quite far away, the oldest son of a poor family that is bleeding itself white to pay for his apprenticeship. Despite the fact that—for the time being—Vito has only practiced the use of the broom. That's the custom, even though the novice is relegated the most thankless tasks for the first few years, he must pay for his upkeep.

The girls at the convent sometimes used to ask me to tell them about life in the studio.

"It's just like life on a farm," I would explain to them, "except that instead of milking the cows, we grind colors. Instead of churning the butter, we mix siccatives. Instead of cutting up rabbits to sell at the market, we cut them up to make glue, animal glue. Otherwise, it's exactly the same. We all live together, we take our meals together. An apprentice is the equivalent of a menial farmhand and, for the major works, students are hired. On the farm, they would be called day laborers. And then there is the senior assistant, he's sort of like a foreman.

With a wink of the eye I'd go on, "At times, just as on a farm, the foreman ends up marrying the farmer's daughter. . . . Except when his name is Roberto," I would add with a laugh, "and he happens to be a despicable little pest, and as ugly as sin."

My life at the convent already seems so far behind me!

However, tomorrow will soon be here, and I need to be up before the cock's crow.

6

Not getting enough sleep generally leaves me feeling exhilarated, at least in the morning. Afternoons, I usually end up dropping with fatigue.

For the time being, I'm still feeling fine.

A touch of red ochre. I wipe off my brush. Mute the color with the ends of the bristles . . .

In the model's absence, I'll have to rely upon my memory. I am guided as much by my mind's eye as by my father's preliminary sketches. I do my best to bring out the man's vanity; his features exude an air of self-satisfaction. He'll be delighted to find that it resembles him even more.

During the portrait sittings he had irritated me, but now, seeing him standing there cockily on the canvas leaning against my easel, stuffed into a suit of shining armor that has probably never been near a battle, with chin uplifted as if he were the very prince of this world, I find him truly grotesque.

Papa gave me permission to finish this portrait. It's the first time that he's placed so much confidence in me. I'm adding the last highlights, bursts of white or Naples yellow. The client had worn a gilt-colored suit of armor, but I decided to make it silver, like the scales of those fish that Fulvio had tried to give me. Papa approved of my decision.

If I could, I would paint a big red nose on his face. But my father wouldn't appreciate it; clients are to be treated with respect.

Oh, here comes Papa now, accompanied by a tall, muscular fisherman.

Good heavens! How handsome he is! Where did my father dig that one up?

Orazio shows him the accessories. "The shield in the right hand," he explains, "and the upraised sword in the left . . . Flex your knee just a bit more . . . Perfect, get undressed."

So, today there will be a nude study.

"Tuzia," my father orders, "have the curtain put up for Artemisia."

My stepmother diligently hurries to draw the heavy canvas curtain that separates me from the platform where the model is going to pose. She takes the opportunity to examine the young man's anatomy with a look of admiration.

That blasted curtain again! It infuriates me to be treated like a chaste little virgin. I throw my paintbrush down in a rage. "I'll never be able to improve if you forbid me to paint male nudes!"

My father loses his temper in turn. "Artemisia! I am not the one who decided to make it an offense for women to study anatomy—it was the Pope himself."

I retort that he should inform the sovereign pontiff that his absurd decree bars me from half of the world of painting.

"Come now, Misia," he insists, curbing his impatience, "you know what the penalty is . . . Do you really want to go to prison?"

Tuzia butts in with a sugary voice, "Unless it is your father you wish to send to prison?"

Let them go and shut themselves up with men only in their man's world, if that's what they want! Patience! The day will come when the most beautiful young men in all of Italy will be begging to pose in the nude for me.

Flinging myself at the curtain, I hastily sketch out the contours of the model that are silhouetted on the canvas.

"If that's the way things are," I say, finishing the rough sketch, "I'll just take what little there is!" And I stomp furiously away, without looking back, shouting at my father, "You can finish the portrait on your own!"

What's come over me? Why these sudden fits of temper? Where is the veil of self-composure I had learned to hang over my face so well in the convent?

I'm so impulsive . . . The exact opposite of Papa, whom I hardly understand anyway. To myself, I call him The Mask.

Externally, he displays such evenness of character, patience, and benevolence, and yet all of these things are contradicted when his speech problems crop up every now and again. My father sometimes stutters when things do not go as he would like. People say that it's due to a malformation of the vocal chords. I don't believe that. I think that in truth, a great lump of anxiety gets stuck in his throat, only letting out words in fits and starts, and that it reveals his inner turmoil. I can sense an incredible violence in him, all the more threatening because it is contained. Sometimes I wish he would break loose, just explode once and for all. For example, he could beat the daylights out of my stepmother, who well deserves it, or trip up a clumsy apprentice.

I don't know . . . He could give me a good slap in the face when I start acting cantankerous like I did a little while ago.

He needs to find some way. He never expresses his feelings, except when he's painting.

I sometimes spend hours before his paintings, not only admiring them, but attempting to decipher, behind the colorful shapes, my father's true character. I can recognize, lying below the features of his subjects, the multitude of faces that are hidden beneath his own. I concentrate, superimpose all of these faces, and suddenly the painting becomes frightening to look at.

Papa told me briefly about his unhappy childhood in a village not far from Rome. It helped me to understand him a little better.

He was an only child. His father, the town's sole notary, was endowed with such a bulging stomach that he had a concave desk built especially to make room for his paunch. He loved to eat so much that his wife had sewn two large oilcloth pouches on either side of his doublet. Every morning, she would fill the pouch on the right with pastries and sweets and the pouch on the left with garlic bread and crackers.

One day, a horse drawing a cart had bolted, running down the alley where my grandfather was walking, on his way to call on one of his clients. The fat man plastered his back against the wall to escape the collision—and the enormous protruding belly was lopped off like head by a guillotine.

Papa was five years old. His mother, a very devout woman, never re-married. She dug up and revived an archaic custom according to which a male child whose father is deceased, should spend the better part of his time in the company of the dead, keeping the deathwatch, following the funeral processions barefooted, and praying over their graves so that their souls may rest in peace.

Everyone called Papa "The Cemetery Boy."

A friend of the family, the agent for a famous Roman painter, took pity on the little boy who always dressed in black and never laughed. He asked the lad what his interests were. Orazio answered, "I've grown accustomed to people who don't move. That is why I love painting so much. The subjects are immobile and yet they aren't dead."

That was how my father was apprenticed to the painter and quickly demonstrated true artistic talent.

It is simply pure chance that has brought Papa this far. And here I am, throwing fits because things are moving so slowly for me. Perhaps in reality things are going too fast. Not so very long ago, I was shut up in the cloister, waiting for some unknown husband chosen by my father to come and rescue me. I would simply have been casting off one yoke to take on another.

So I should be grateful and happily accept the circumstances; allow myself to evolve over time, stop being such a spoiled brat. I need to beat that old adage into my head: "Speed is one thing, haste another," I know that I'm very privileged. Doesn't my father allow me to work on his paintings? And neither is he unaware that I take crayons and paper to my room and draw until late into the night. Doesn't he look the other way? Doesn't he allow me to run wild as the wind through the dunes without pinning me down with a chaperone?

I think about all of these things while walking along on the beach, which is deserted in the midday heat. Unmanned boats lie helplessly on their sides, even the seagulls have found refuge elsewhere. I always come here when I need to think things over. The damp sand sticks to the hem at the back of my dress, weighing it down. I feel as though I have a long train and smile to myself, thinking: "So that's it, you think you're some sort of princess!"

Yet I don't have a very high opinion of myself. Especially not today.

Skimming along horizontally over the sand, whisking the few dry, stinging grains along with it, a hot wind blows, blasts . . . pants and groans. That the wind should blow and blast is normal enough, but should it pant and groan? I listen more closely: the odd music seems to be coming from some rocks overhead. An evil spirit? A beast of some sort? A wounded beast perhaps? I run over and scale the tall rocks.

What I see makes me duck for shelter. What I see makes my heart beat even faster. Wide-eyed, I watch.

They are naked on the sand of the creek. A man and a woman. The woman is lying on her back, her legs are spread apart. Between her loins, the man is frenetically grinding away.

I recognize the woman; it's our Saint Cecilia of yesterday.

She seems to be in pain, her face is completely contorted from the force of the onslaught. But no, now she's laughing. A short, silent laugh, that brings a bit of saliva to the corners of her mouth.

These are the emotions that my father should attempt to capture. Carnal ecstasy. Although the man is well rooted in the woman, he seems to have left her now and is finishing the race on his own, giving sharp little yelping cries. He drives faster and faster until he suddenly collapses and falls silent.

Now he is helping Saint Cecilia to get up. Gently he brushes off her hair, her shoulders, and the back of her legs to rid them of the mixture of sand and sweat sticking to the skin. The lovers dress hurriedly and leave the creek holding hands. When they reach the top of the rocky outcrop, where man's territory begins, their fingers unlock.

The deep hollows left by the buttocks, the lighter marks of the arms, the shoulders the heels. The sand in those traces is warmer, damper too. I scoop up a handful of the sand; it's as if it were permeated with the sap of life. I sniff it; there's no particular odor. Or yes, there is. It smells of the cellar. The cellar that frightens me so every time they send me down to fetch some wine. Wine is drunkenness. The cellar is the un-known. I feel frightened of being drawn into drunkenness and the un-known, panicked at what I've just seen and knowing that one day it will surely happen to me . . . Bewildered too.

I'm overcome with confused feelings. I'm too hot, I'm too cold. My body shrinks and is too small for me. The next minute it is floating boundlessly about me. What is that warm bubble glowing in my ab-domen, fluttering up, subsiding, swirling around like a mad sun?

I'm lying down in the mark left in sand. My arms, back, and but-tocks fit the hollows left by the young woman's body. With eyes half closed, my limbs are moving ever so slightly. I only just now became aware of it, as if someone else had set me down here without my know-ing it. I look at the sun; it does seem to have gone mad. It's pulsing in rhythm with that bubble in my womb, as if it were inside of me.

I close my eyes; the feeling is still there. I imagine the weight of a body lying upon mine. When I open my eyes, I see nothing but that blazing orb high in the sky.

7

Fitful night. Voluptuous dreams.

The last one is so powerful, I awaken with a start.

I am not met with the pale light of dawn. Why is the sunshine already playing upon my stained-glass windows? I throw them open. The sun is already high in the sky.

Why didn't anyone wake me? I pull on my apprentice's trousers so hurriedly that I get both of my legs in the same hole and nearly fall flat on my face. Now the shirt, quick. Forget about the turban! Opening the door, I run smack into Tuzia, who is holding a beautiful yellow silk dress in her hands. Well, well! She's put on some makeup today, and she's even wearing jewelry! What's all this about?

"Hurry up, put this on!" she snaps, laying the dress on my bed. "And fix up your hair a bit."

Oh no! Not today! I'm in too much of a hurry to get to work.

So I complain in an irritated voice, that it isn't fair, that I have a lot of work to do, that I can't do everything, that I'm sick of having to replace models that cancel their sitting.

Tuzia curtly interrupts my diatribe, "Hurry up now, everyone is waiting for you."

And indeed, they are waiting for me.

They're sitting around the kitchen tables stuffing themselves with plump little cakes oozing with unctuous cream.

I recognize the gentleman first. It's our former apothecary from the via della Croce. Business is thriving from what I can see. The old vulture has put on some flesh, his brocade vest looks as if it's about to split.

On the other hand, his wife hasn't got any fatter, just a lot more wrinkled. Peering over her cake, she scrutinizes me.

Ah, I hadn't noticed the young man . . . Tuzia motions for me to sit down next to him on the bench. Only one thought comes to my mind, "Stop staring at me in that way, it feels as if you'll suck me right up with that look. Actually, you seem quite nice. A little foolish perhaps, but nice . . ."

The lady opens her mouth and yet she doesn't stick her cake in it. In that case she must be intending to say something. She addresses Tuzia, rather than me. "I don't approve of a young woman devoting herself to painting, it really isn't a proper pastime, but my son insisted. I finally agreed to order a portrait of him to be painted by Artemisia."

What are they talking about? Who are they trying to fool?

Tuzia smiles at the son and assures him that I will be very honored. "Isn't that so, Artemisia?"

Then she adds, baring her blackened eyeteeth, "A portrait! What better way to get to know each another?"

That's exactly what I thought, they want to marry me off to that poor boy . . . I'd rather die, he's much too ugly! And I haven't the slightest desire to get married, anyway. Now they're really at it, they're broaching the subject of my dowry.

I have to find a way to parry.

First, I squint at my fiancé's face as I've seen people do with animals in the marketplace. Score one, it makes him uncomfortable!

Then I suddenly grab his chin and turn his head to the side, pursing my lips dubiously as I examine his profile.

He seems to be afraid that I'll strike him.

Now everyone is watching.

At this very moment, I choose to ask his mother coolly, "Could he pose in the nude?"

Tuzia's hand has just come furiously down upon my cheek. The slap makes me smile, my victory certainly didn't cost me much.

They are leaving the table—the mother with her arm around her son. A mother hen and her chick!

Tuzia is trying to make them stay, "Please excuse Artemisia, she's just a child, she doesn't know what she's saying . . . She's been so hard to manage since her mother's death."

They are already out in the courtyard. I can vaguely hear the mother consoling her son, telling him that it's no wonder, a woman painter, she'd warned him. . . .

Yes, she's right, it's totally unheard of. And I'm certainly not going to stop now, not after getting off to such an auspicious start!

I'm still wearing the yellow silk dress. It is sweeping me along the path to the cave like a bright sail. Apart from Fulvio and myself, no one has ever explored the depths of the cavern. People say that it is inhabited by evil spirits. The entrance resembles a tortured mouth. No one ever ventures in there. Fishermen make the sign of the cross when passing the threshold.

I'm almost certain that I'll find my friend there. That's where he always goes to mend his nets, think things over, or take a little nap. And fondle himself sometimes too. I caught him at it once and he was really angry. He wouldn't let me go near him for a week! He won't run away this time.

Despite being in a hurry, I'm inching along slowly, with my hands outstretched to avoid bumping into the limestone stalactites. Even though I'm familiar with this place—I used to play here as a child with Fulvio—each time I come here. I am still filled with a fear that is a mixture of dread and excitement.

I'm through the narrow stone gullet, I'm in the monster's stomach.

Fulvio is sitting with his back turned to me, resplendent in the ray of light spilling down from one of the open chimneys. He's mending his fishnet and his ragged shirt reveals little patches of skin in places. Beading with sweat, his muscles bulge in cadence with the thick curved needle that plunges into the needlework of cords.

Fulvio didn't hear me come up. I left my shoes at the entrance to the cave, hidden in the weeds, to better savor the cold moistness of the sand. I don't know, maybe in hopes of surprising him too. I'm only ten strides away from him now. Five. Three. One.

My fingers touch the skin of his shoulder, exposed by a tear in his shirt. It is warm, very smooth and a little moist. He doesn't start. Was he waiting for me?

I take a deep breath and blurt out all at once: "Fulvio, if I let you kiss me, would you do a favor for me afterward?"

"If you want me to, yes . . ."

"Then kiss me."

I close my eyes. His lips seek mine. Our mouths press against each other. Fulvio breaks through the barrier of my teeth. So, when lovers kiss, they roll their tongues? I like the smell he exhales from his nostrils in quick snorts—a mysterious aroma, somewhat sweet, coming from inside his body. Fulvio grabs my wrists. I pull gently away, lay my hand on his burning cheek.

"Get undressed," I say gently.

He quickly unlaces his shirt. I'd like to be inside his mind. What is a man's desire like? Do they have a glowing bubble in their abdomen also?

A tanned chest, already muscular. Arms that wish to enfold me. I pull away and murmur, "Take off your trousers."

Now he's getting self-conscious, looking a little awkward. Maybe because it is I who am giving the orders? The trousers slip noiselessly to the sand. Now Fulvio has nothing on but a sort of loincloth knotted at the sides. He's waiting.

"Take everything off. Even that," I say, pointing to the bit of fabric. "It makes a white mark that breaks the line of the body.

He obeys, unties the knots. The cloth remains suspended to his erect penis for a moment, like a coat on a hook. Feeling a little uncomfortable, I look away and take some paper and red clay crayons from my satchel.

Fulvio quickly covers his sex with his hands and stares incredulously, shamefacedly at the material that I am setting out on a low rock.

"Are you going to draw me?"

I don't answer, walk over to him and kneel down.

"You see how this muscle in your back stretches down across your flank to join the muscle in your thigh?" I ask, following in amazement the contours of the dense volumes with my hand. That's barely visible in women.

"Let me see," Fulvio pleads in a choked voice.

I shake my head, going "*shshsh shsh*," and tell him to keep quiet and stay put. It's the first time I've ever really seen a man naked.

With eyes half closed, I sit down at his feet and let my fingers explore the unknown, run over the surface of the infinite possibilities I'm suddenly discovering. I try to memorize everything. The legs are long, firm, straighter than a woman's. The buttocks are harder, higher set, and rather small, there is a slight hollow in either side before they bulge back out toward the hips. The geography of the male body being unfamiliar to me, my hands go astray, touch something soft, slimy, covered with hair. I open my eyes: it's those fleshy pouches hanging under his penis. Stallions, bulls, and male dogs have the same. They say that it's an essential part of procreation. They cut those of bulls off to make oxen of them.

In any case, the contact seems to have considerable effect on Fulvio. He pulls me to my feet and draws me over to him.

"No! You're not to move! You promised. Let me do as I please . . ."

An hour later, I've finished my drawings.

8

Two little dogs come running into the studio, yapping authoritatively. They are shiny-coated and wear collars studded with precious gems. Dogs that obviously belong to some rich person, dragging in their wake a liveried manservant. The master of the trio appears, I recognize the man in the portrait who is sporting a wide ruff of pleated cloth today, just like a Spaniard. It makes him look like a poor neckless creature.

Hidden behind an arras, I observe him whipping at the air with his crop. "Signor Orazio!" he screeches in a thin, falsetto voice. "Signor Orazio!"

Papa and Roberto come scurrying up. They must have been expecting this visit, for they are dressed in their best attire.

With a snap of his fingers, Roberto motions the apprentices to clear out.

I'm well hidden, no one has seen me.

Papa leads the man over to the portrait, draped with a square piece of velvet, and slowly unveils the painting.

Our client steps up to it, sniffs at the paint, takes three steps backward, studies his image as if in a mirror, steps back further, chin in hand, then announces, "You've surpassed yourself, Master Gentileschi. Very impressive, really . . . It is alive, powerful . . . Superb."

Affecting the air of a connoisseur, he adds, "No one has your sense of color."

I giggle happily behind my arras because I'm the one who chose the colors. Even coming from an ignoramus, it's a pleasing compliment.

My father has caught sight of me. He bows with deep reverence and casts a knowing wink in my direction.

"I'm very honored."

The client then purses his lips. "Still," and after an interminable silence, "Still, I am surprised that you chose to paint the armor silver. I was wearing a gilt suit of armor during the sitting."

Here we go, he's going to start quibbling. And I start mimicking him back in my corner, which nearly makes my father burst out laughing.

Orazio regains his self-control. "I'm well aware of that, sir. But I wanted this portrait to be timeless, a balance of colors that could defy the onslaughts of time, and the changing fashions."

The knight nods his head and his chest swells. With a look of approval, he agrees, "Yes indeed, and I believe that it was I myself who suggested the change."

"There's no question about it, sir. Your advice has always helped me to improve my work." Unfortunately, my father adds, "Also, silver brings out your true stature, makes you seem taller . . ."

"Silver, eh?"

The knight solemnly holds out a purse to his valet, who hands it to Roberto, who hands it to my father.

"Have the canvas delivered before Friday," he says as he walks toward the door. "I'm giving a banquet and I would like to show it to my friends."

His face is expressionless.

"As for the question of stature," he adds abruptly, "my symbol is gold, not silver. So don't forget to replace the silver with a nice yellow gold."

Roberto shows them to the door. My father remains alone, standing dejectedly before the painting. I come out from behind the tapestry, waving my arms about in indignation.

He speaks of color as if it were a matter of matching his stockings to his breeches!"

Papa tucks a strand of hair that has escaped from my turban back behind my ear. "But whom do we work for, my dear?"

I straighten myself up proudly. "I paint for myself!"

"No, painters work for those who have the means to pay for their services," he declares in a voice slack with resignation.

He hugs me very tightly in his arms. His wide, stooping back is all I can see over his shoulder. "Never forget, my little sweetheart," he adds, "that under the horrendous gold, our noble silver will always remain."

9

The white house down on the beach has been abandoned for as long
as I can remember. It's a vast building with arcades and thick, notched,
whitewashed walls, pierced by narrow windows like loopholes. It could
easily be mistaken for a naval guardhouse, which it most probably was
in the beginning.

Today, it's ringing with life. Three handcarts are waiting outside the
door, porters are unloading a jumble of odds and ends.

Fulvio and I are burning with curiosity. What's going on? Are there
new neighbors moving in? Who would ever want to live in a house so
near the sea? Certainly not a family of fishermen, they don't like the
immutable panorama of waves. They prefer little village cottages, well
protected from the unfettered elements. Or else, if they sometimes build
a house near the dunes, their windows all deliberately face away from
the water, to keep out the sea breezes. Perhaps for a change of scenery?

We run down to the beach, intrigued by the richly embroidered tent
pitched in the sand.

A handsome man with a jet-black beard comes out from under the
pavilion, followed by four young men, all dressed in the Florentine
fashion.

The man is standing there straight as a pole, a purple cape floating
down from his shoulders. He emanates an innate sense of command.
He is calling out orders, but the wind blowing in the opposite direction prevents me from hearing. How old could he be? Thirty, forty?

Aha! So, he's a painter . . .

Each in turn, his assistants are setting things up for him in the sand, one brings out a box full of paintbrushes, another a white canvas on an easel, the third assistant is carrying pots of ground-up pigment, and the fourth, a wooden frame divided into squares by wires strung tightly across it, and a long stick that ends in a sort of eyepiece. My father has a similar set of equipment. It's called a perspective frame.

Two helpers go back into the tent, they come back out holding two perfectly scaled-down models of boats, shorter than a child's arm. They set the toys on a tripod in front of the perspective frame, with the sea in the background.

A group of onlookers, peasants and fishermen, are milling about the unwonted event. A fat woman laughs, covering her mouth with her hand, the youngsters elbow one another. Hardly anyone says a word, they simply stand there watching, with stupid smiles on their faces.

I'm taking it all in with wide-eyed fascination, not daring to get too close.

Indifferent to all of the attention he is drawing, the man sits down at his easel and, with quick lines, begins to sketch onto the canvas the models of the galleons that seem so very real with the blue water dancing in the distance. He leaves the easel frequently to go and look through the eyepiece that stands a few feet in front of the frame, whose gridlines divide the landscape into regular squares.

"He's out in the open air," Fulvio comments, "and yet he looks through a window!"

"Keep quiet, you're so silly!"

Angered by my repartee and by my unconstrained interest in the painter, Fulvio is resentful. "The sea is too large to fit into such a small canvas. And anyway, I bet he doesn't know the first thing about boats!"

To tell the truth, I'm completely stupefied myself. Painting out-of-doors! No one ever heard of such a thing!

"Doesn't he even have a studio?" I wonder aloud, without really expecting an answer.

For a very long time, I observe the painter at work, incapable of tearing my eyes from those ships that now seem to be floating on the canvas.

Most of the curiosity seekers left sometime ago.

I don't miss a single step of his technique. If I dared, I'd go up to the handsome painter and give him a piece of my mind for using a thick white primer to bring out the light; I find the device just a bit too facile.

The sun is setting out on the horizon. The deep voice of the man makes me jump with surprise. "That's enough for today, Batisto, the light has changed. All right, let's pack everything up!"

He calls out to Fulvio who is sitting on the sand. "You, young fisherman! The south wind is up, you won't be catching any fish now. Come over and give us a hand, you'll earn a good tip."

Fulvio jumps to his feet, proud to have been noticed. He lifts a trunk that is heavier than himself and staggers off after the suite of attendants.

One of the assistants, the one who is carrying the wet painting, trips. His master catches him up by the ear. "Careful there! Capturing the details of a landscape doesn't mean getting sand stuck all over the canvas!"

I watch the strange procession slowly moving away. They're walking toward the white house on the beach, all loaded down like so many mules.

The master is leading the way, walking along with his hands in his pockets. I find him as dashing as a conquistador.

I feel that I've learned something today, but what exactly I'm not sure . . .

10

Papa and I spend the morning looking through the drawings I've done since I came back to live with him. I'm already aware that these hours alone with him will be unforgettable. We discuss each line of my drawings, interspersing discussions about art in general with talk of our plans for the future.

My father dreams of our working together forever. "We'll go a long way, my girl," he says. "Together, we'll discover new ways of rendering colors, new techniques for treating light, new rules of composition. We'll work as a team on the major pieces, just as the great masters do, and we'll sign with just one name: Gentileschi! God willing, we'll found a new school of painting."

Taking my hands firmly in his, he adds, "And you'll give me a passel of grandchildren whom we'll put right to work and who will carry on our fine family tradition."

For the first time in my life I feel as though I'm truly being treated as an equal.

For an instant, I almost think I'll show him the nudes I did of Fulvio in the cave, which I keep hidden under a loose floorboard. But no, he wouldn't understand. Not yet.

Orazio puts the drawings he's selected into a large portfolio. He's also chosen the dress I am to wear. A modest, loose-fitting dress. And the way in which I'll wear my hair. Two braids wound around my crown. No makeup. He wants me to be as simple as possible. I mustn't draw too much attention where we are going today. It's a place from which women are banned.

Papa is taking me to the Academy of San Luca—Saint Luke is the patron saint of artists—in hopes that I will be accepted as a student there.

The carriage carries us at a swift gallop through the streets of Rome and jolts around so terribly that it hurts my breasts. Laughing, I hold them pressed against my chest.

This is the most wonderful day of my life.

We drive from one end of the city to the other. There are new churches under construction almost everywhere. I wave at my old neighbors from the via della Croce. I even happen to catch sight of Isabella, the whitener's daughter. She looks as if she might go into labor any minute, is dragging two little tykes after her and carrying a tub full of putrid hides on her head. To think that she's the same age as I . . . Thank heavens my father is a painter rather than a tanner!

We drive around the impressive Bernini statue that so elegantly adorns the center of the square and pull to a stop in front of the austere walls of the Academy. I'm not laughing anymore. I'm a little frightened.

My father and I strike out amid the gray marble pillars under the arcades, feeling the intrigued and mocking eyes of students upon us. Many of them nudge each other and whisper upon seeing the green portfolio I'm carrying under my arm.

Feeling quite intimidated, I stick close to the walls that are covered with paintings and where the recent endeavors of students hang side by side with copies and original works of the masters. I'm torn between the desire to examine each work in detail and the irrepressible urge to move on to the next painting.

A representation of *Judith Decapitating Holofernes* is breathtaking. "You are standing before one of the works of the great Caravaggio, my child. He's a master from Naples, I once studied under him."

I am awestruck. My fingers follows the lines of the faces without touching them. "Look, Papa, he painted each fold in the flesh, each wrinkle . . ."

Orazio nods his head. "He invented a new procedure. Caravaggio developed the idea of sitting his models in a dark room and hanging a light high above them that would illuminate the main parts of the body and leave the rest in shadow. That is why there are such sharp contrasts in his work."

"How intensely real the people look!"

There's a vague bitterness in Papa's smile. "He is also the first person to have refused to paint idealized figures, with perfect features. Instead he uses people he finds in the streets, in wash-houses, or in cabarets as models. His virgins, his Magus, and even his representations of the infant Jesus seem to have been fashioned by life, by its burdens and by its joys."

And he goes on, "Biblical figures with wrinkles and imperfections aren't to everyone's liking. It has already caused Caravaggio quite a few problems."

I point out the blade cutting into Holofernes' throat. "He's more familiar with people than with beasts! The day I saw a pig being slaughtered, I can assure you, there was blood gushing everywhere. Here you'd think that Judith was cutting into a slice of bread!"

Orazio leads me away by the arm. "Hush, Misia. Sometimes, one can say too much about a painting. Just be grateful that he has inspired you to attempt to surpass him one day."

Papa asked me to wait on the terrace while he was negotiating my admission with the director of the Academy. I'm sitting on an elaborately decorated marble bench facing the door to the office; from time to time, I dart an anxious glance inside. My father walks straight over to a man sitting behind a wide, inlaid wooden desk. All I can see of the man is the stiff upper portion of his body. "I've brought you the drawings, my good sir," says my father, after greeting him politely.

"Your daughter's drawings, yes, I know."

Orazio launches into his appeal, claiming that I'm a genius in his opinion, that my talent far excels that of everyone else in his studio. He unties the portfolio and pulls out the drawings one by one. "See for yourself . . ."

The director barely deigns to look at them. He seems terribly embarrassed.

"A promising talent, indeed," he stammers awkwardly. "But . . ."

"Note the innate sense of movement, the grace, the harmony!"

"True, but . . ."

"And this foreshortening, not one of my students has Artemisia's ability to . . ."

"Please understand, master, no one could come more highly recommended than by Orazio Gentileschi . . . Try to understand—there is no place for a young woman at the Academy."

Papa pounds his fist down on the desk, and begins stuttering, "I tell you that she paints as well as a man . . ."

The director interrupts him, "But she is not a man!"

The show is over. My father can try to negotiate till he's blue in the face, I know that the curtain has fallen. Tears come flooding to my eyes and at first I don't notice the two students who are walking around me, making faces and little obscene noises.

One of them leers at me: "Are we lost, my little sweet?"

The other asks, "What are you doing here? Have you come to meet your fiancé?" He swanks about with his fly front almost touching my nose. "If you're interested in painters, perhaps the two of us can do business together . . ."

I jump to my feet and slap him across the face with all my might.

The noise alerts my father, who rushes out and, seeing the student holding his cheek, says in a voice oozing with affected civility, "Allow me to introduce myself, Orazio Gentileschi."

"I've studied your work, master, and I greatly admire it," the young lout answers respectfully.

"I believe I'm familiar with you too," says my father plastering his forehead up against the student's. Grabbing hold of the boy's genitals, he adds, "And if you are a student here, you only have these to thank for it!" He squeezes until the youth screams in pain. "So take care not to lose them!" Orazio hisses vehemently.

As we walk out of the Academy, I force myself to keep my head held very high.

Being turned away from the Academy has deeply shaken me. I'd truly believed I would be admitted. I had prepared myself for a complete change of lifestyle, and now here I am right back where I started from. My whole being was stretching toward the future. Will I now have to close the door on all my dreams? Never!

An idea has been running around in my mind ever since this morning. What if I were to do the same thing as the Florentine down on the beach? Perhaps it is not so difficult to paint out-of-doors. At least it's novel.

I drag a heavy armchair out into the garden and put it in the shade with its back to the dunes, facing the wooded hills. With a piece of charcoal in one hand, a sheet of paper on my knees, I set to work, but I am soon out of my depth.

Orazio and Roberto are watching me from the wide-opened window. "What are you up to out there?" asks my father.

"I'm drawing, as you can well see."

Orazio shrugs his shoulders and turns toward Roberto. "Why is she working out in a field like a peasant woman? What is she drawing? Nothing will come of all of this." Then he adds, "Painting out-of-doors, what a curious idea!"

Roberto sniggers, "It's the latest fashion in Florence, from what I've heard. Also, one of the children from the village just informed me that Agostino Tassi arrived in the area yesterday. I would guess that your daughter probably ran across him painting one of those well-known seascapes of his, and that now she's trying to imitate him."

"Tassi is already here? And you're just now telling me about it? You'll have to take him a note of welcome, we must strike up a good relationship with him, we're to begin on our joint work in a few days."

Is that so? The painter from the beach and my father will soon be

working together? Undoubtedly one of those frescoes for Monte Cavallo's church, which Nicolo, my father's agent, mentioned on his last
visit. I know that father met with the head of the diocese afterward, but
he didn't tell me what had been discussed. He simply said, "You will
soon be working on your first major fresco, my dear. I'll leave all of the
cherubim in the centerpiece for you to paint, and even two saints!"

I had leapt up and cried out in delight, hopping about holding one
of my feet, as if the overwhelming joy had somehow hurt me.

That day Papa had spoken of another painter from Florence, who
was to work in collaboration with him to bring the vast project to
fruition. I hadn't retained his name. Now that I know, I find it difficult
to imagine Agostino Tassi painting anything other than boats.

I may be critical, but I must admit I don't have anywhere near his
talent for painting from nature. How in the world does he do it? I labor over the paper, crumpling up several sheets before I can even obtain an approximate sketch of the main elements in the landscape on
either side of the horizon.

My drawing is worthless. It is decidedly less complicated to paint the
human figure with the shaded and the light areas clearly defined in the
candlelight. With the green of the hills, one can't really tell where it begins or where it ends. How disorganized all this lush greenness is, and
they say that each leaf, each branch, each flower is the work of God. He
must have quite a sense of perspective and a wonderful pair of eyes! All
I can see is a magma of vegetation from which no volumes emerge. I
don't know how to draw things that are indistinct, I can't tell what comes
before or after. And anyway, the trees are so full of detail, the lighting
is too playful, too changeable.

I give up trying to paint the sunlight; yes, for the time being, I give up.

But I'm not renouncing the idea of painting elsewhere. I've had more
than enough of Roberto's comments and Tuzia's constant supervision.
I'm going to build my own studio. I want to be more independent.

Papa has gone off on horseback to pay the notorious Agostino Tassi
a call. I take the opportunity to go and find Fulvio along with two of

his fishermen friends. Even my little Marco comes and helps to build a wooden frame for my shelter. As a covering, I use the hideous tarpaulin upon which I'd sketched the contours of a male nude because I'd been forbidden to see the model.

Tuzia attempts to rip the heavy curtain out of my arms. "What do you plan on doing with that now?"

I don't even bother to answer her.

Fulvio, his friends, and I unfold the thick canvas and drape it over the framework. Marco, with all the eager enthusiasm of boyhood, busies himself pounding pegs into the ground to secure the tarp. How I love that child! I wish I could spend more time with him!

"Fulvio," I say, "try to arrange things so that I can adjust the lighting according to the time of day. I want to be able to pull one side of the tent up or down, as needed."

We bring a few pieces of furniture over from Papa's studio, a rack for holding canvases, an easel, and some painting materials.

Tuzia has reached the end of her patience. "Your father will never allow this!"

I'm carrying a tall mirror into the studio and, without really intending to, I bump into her quite violently. She squeals like a mouse who's just had its tail stepped on. "Orazio will make you take it all down when he comes home!"

I see the reflection of her face in the mirror, rage and pain distorting her features. The vision is unpleasant so I tilt the mirror slightly and it turns into a thousand different paintings as I walk along, reflecting patches of sky, a flower bed, a distant landscape . . .

Finally, my own studio, even though it does look a bit odd, with one of the tent flaps displaying a charcoal sketch of a male silhouette.

I immediately close myself up to begin a self-portrait. I draw what the mirror reflects: a young woman leaning forward—the soft lines of her throat disappearing gracefully into a plunging neckline—with an uplifted paintbrush. The painting slowly takes on form, and for the first time in my life, I recognize myself. Body and soul are finally reconciled.

I I

Little Vito is my protégé, but sometimes he is also my spy. The child is always either sweeping up or washing the paintbrushes. He sees and hears everything that goes on. He's the one who took the apprentices' lunch over to the work site. He's just returned from the Monte Cavallo church and I'm asking him if the teamwork between my father and the painter from the beach seems to be off to a promising start. The boy has a real gift for imitation. He reports everything to me, never forgetting a single sentence or detail.

"So, Vito, how was it?"

"Wait a minute, Artemisia, let me start from the beginning. First of all, Tassi's and your father's apprentices set up the scaffolding and all the equipment. There was quite a crowd, I can tell you. And a hellish lot of noise. In the meanwhile, the masters were discussing matters very loudly."

And he launches into an imitation, miming each person, changing places every few seconds. "First Batisto, Tassi's assistant, brought in the models. Those women were stark naked!" He motions in the air with his hands tracing implicitly feminine shapes. "When he saw the first model, Tassi simply said, 'Too thin.' Then Batisto lined up two others that his master thoroughly looked over. Then still another that had kept on a scanty pair of drawers that Tassi wanted removed immediately."

Vito steps to the side and assumes an uncanny resemblance to my father when he is angry. "Orazio grumbled that he had already done full scale drawings, and therefore they had no need for models."

Taking a swaggering stance to depict the vain Tassi, Vito responds,

"Gentileschi, you know perfectly well that I will be doing the central composition. The Pope named me master of the project."

At this, I interrupt Vito, "What's that, he's doing the central composition? And what of my cherubim? And my two saints? Papa promised me!"

Vito quickly reassures me, saying the two men began to bicker like a couple of children, and Orazio insisted it was he who had first been chosen to paint the fresco.

"Then Tassi said, 'Are we here to discuss the past or the future?' Recovering his temper, he went on to promise your father they would do magnificent work together."

Vito bursts out laughing. "He's really very funny. Do you know what he said to Orazio? That one day people would recognize Tassi and Gentilischi as truly great artists . . . and only a practiced connoisseur would be able to affirm, in seeing the finished frescoes, that Tassi was just a little bit greater than Gentileschi. Your father answered with a laugh that he believed he would survive this partnership."

Vito puts his arm around me as if I were Orazio and he, Tassi. "Come now, Gentileschi," the boy whispers, affecting a gruff voice, "let's go to the brothel together. We can share a girl and divide the job up between us just as we do here . . ."

Your father replied, "Oh no! Painting celestial breasts by day and petting earthly ones by night! No thank you, Tassi, I'll leave the night work up to you."

Vito performs a graceful pirouette and takes up his broom again.

While Vito mops the tiled floor, my younger brother plays at jumping over the wet mop each time it passes, laughing himself silly. But I'm not in such a wonderful mood. With clenched fists on my hips, I resolutely await my father's return.

As a matter of fact, here he is now. "Tassi has stolen my angels, Papa!"

Orazio casts a black look at Vito, who suddenly blushes. "I know, Misia, my dear." Is that all he can find to say? I'll surely go mad with despair! "I'm the one who was supposed to paint them, and two of the saints as well!"

"What do you want me to do about it?"

I feel like shaking him. "He steals the work right out from under you nose, and you act as if you don't even notice?"

Before answering, Papa puts on his black smock and sets the wide painter's beret on his head. He sighs. "We should be thankful that we didn't lose the order for the frescoes altogether." He slips on the canvas overshoes. "Tassi has powerful friends in the church," he adds. "People close to the Pope."

Always the same old story. Secret pacts sealed with either money or influence. I'd like to continue to think mine is the most beautiful profession in the world and that I will never let myself get trapped in all of these sordid dealings. The faint voice of reason within me says the contrary. "You'll be just like them, Artemisia."

I compose myself. "Very well," I say, "but at least try and see if he'll agree to doing the nave and let us have the vaults of the transepts."

Orazio seems surprised at my sudden change of heart. He throws my apprentice's garb at me as one would toss a ball to a child and tells me to change in a hurry. We must begin work immediately since the outlines of the figures in the fresco are to be done in the studio.

As I'm running upstairs, Papa stops me in my tracks. "You know, Artemisia, they say that Tassi is a master of perspective. We might very well have something to learn from him. Neither of us can afford to ignore new techniques.

Papa is right. I'm only sixteen and I still have a lot to learn. It could very well be that this Tassi fellow was heaven-sent.

12

All things told, I've ended up getting exactly what I wanted. Papa lets me do quite a bit of the work. He decided that I should be responsible for most of the drawings, that the assistants would transfer them onto the walls of the church, after which he would then lay on the colors and put in the shading. My father won't, however, allow me to work on the scaffolds, partly because he's afraid I'll fall, but also to protect me from Tassi's assistants. Young men from Florence have a bad reputation: they are rumored to be completely lacking in morals.

Fulvio didn't go out to sea today, it was too rough. He's watching me copy over from the original drawing I did yesterday, a representation of Saint Peter who, with the exception of his face, will be entirely hidden in clouds. My friend is curious by nature. He wants me to explain everything I'm doing point by point.

"It's hardly complicated," I say. "First I draw full scale figures on huge pieces of paper; these are called the 'master patterns.' Afterward, I make a tracing—called a 'pouncing pattern'—which I then go back over, perforating the lines with a needle. When the drawing is to be transferred onto the walls of the fresco, someone will hold it up and—so as not to scratch the plaster—pass over the perforations using a soft brush dipped in black powder. Then the paper is removed and my figure drawing simply needs to be filled in a bit, and papa will bring it to life in applying the colors.

I'm not very good at technical explanations, and I lose patience with Fulvio's questions. Especially since he never listens to the answers. He pretends to be snoring, how rude of him! Then he opens one eye and leans over my drawing. "Your Saint Peter's face is too long!" Fulvio says, pulling on his chin and sucking his cheeks in. "He's ludicrous. He looks like a table leg."

It was Fulvio who taught me all about the wind, the sea, and the fish that dwell there, so I'm indebted to him. Holding my temper, I explain, "It's done on purpose. When Saint Peter is perched in his clouds high up on the wall, he'll appear more human. Look . . ." As I tilt the paper, the face, which had been deformed by perspective, recovers it's normal proportions. "See, it will look even shorter when seen from the ground." Mischievously, I whisper in his ear, "It's probably the same when you look at what you've got between your legs . . . In truth, it's a little shorter than what you see in the mirror."

Fulvio jabs me with his elbow and tells me that I'm the one who spends my time looking at myself in mirrors; he knows why I was expelled from the convent, and that he'd seen me gazing at myself in my studio, purportedly in order to paint a self-portrait. Then he adds in an almost nasty tone, "Anyway, what do you know about the body, Artemisia? You're a virgin, aren't you?"

Yes, I'm a virgin, but it is not a permanent state of affairs in a woman's life. I find myself wondering, who will be the first? Perhaps I already know him, perhaps not. For a very long time I thought a prince would come along and carry me away on his white steed. I don't believe in fairy tales any longer, but one never knows.

13

I gulp down a cup of warm milk when I awaken. A little bread and some olives will tide me over till evening time. I've lost weight; my father is worried about me. Personally, I am delighted with the sunken cheeks; they make me look less childlike. At the end of the day, with protective, almost motherly concern, Orazio has someone bring me a bowl of thick soup, doused with oil and enriched with noodles or meat. A few spoonfuls are enough, and I go back to work.

For days now, I haven't left my precious studio. I keep all four flaps of the tent jealously tied shut so I can be alone with my figure drawings. At night, I toss and turn in my bed, and when I don't jump up to jot down my ideas on paper, I continue to draw in my mind.

My fingers are scratched and bloodied from the needles I use to perforate the tracings, and a large callous is beginning to deform the knuckle of the index finger that bears the pressure of the crayons and paintbrushes. I don't mind. I now have ten cartoons completely finished—three muses, five seraphim, and the two saints—John the Baptist and Peter.

With my drawings rolled up in long tubes tucked under my arm, and the same modest dress that I wore the day I went to the Academy hanging loosely about my body, I walk quickly through the fields. The atmosphere is oppressive. The air is muggy, laden with the damp warmth of July mornings. I feel as if I'm suffocating, and so I speed up my pace to try to create a bit of a breeze on my face.

As I run along, the dress clings to the front of my body, billows out behind. The air caresses my willowy frame under the cloth and whistles through the tubes of paper with the little hooting sound of an owl. I must look like some strange kind of bird, flapping its wings but unable to take flight.

And yet, in my mind, I'm flying quite high. The frustration I've been feeling from keeping my work secret, combined with my happiness now at finally being ready to show it to Papa, have given me wings. Today is Sunday, the assistants' day off, but I'm sure Orazio will be at the work site.

The petals of umbellifers adhere to my white dress, like little bursts of light. I cross a field of sunflowers and now am finally in the pine forest that skirts this side of Monte Cavallo's church. I dash through the trees as rapidly as I can and, for the first time, I don't even notice the beauty around me, the silver sunbeams playing in the branches, the sparrows flitting about, the sparkling wet dewdrops bejewling my ankles.

If Fulvio saw me racing along like this, as if the devil were after me, he'd certainly make fun of me. "Oh-ho, Artemisia, afraid of the big bad wolf?" Fulvio is so silly, he's always joking around. He acts like we're still children. Except when it comes to lovemaking. For that, he'd rather have me grow up faster.

The shape of the church appears through a break in the wood, its new golden dome contrasts sharply with the almost black-green of the surrounding trees. Finally, my feet leave the soft carpet of pine needles to trod upon a patch of yellowing stubby grass, it's as if it had been worn away under the feet of a multitude of Sunday worshippers.

I slow down, catch my breath.

The heavy wooden door is open. Upon stepping over the threshold, a suffocating smell of siccatives catches in my throat. Despite the overall disorder inside this church, the lack of incense, a priest, or liturgical music, it remains nonetheless the house of God. I enter in silence, not forgetting to touch my forehead with holy water from the nearly dry basin before making the sign of the cross.

I glance around looking for my father, to no avail.

There is only a young man dressed in workclothes standing with his back to me. He is slinging plaster onto the wall with a trowel. Intrigued, I watch his sure, regular movements. My father's lessons on the art of frescoes come back to me almost word for word. "First, a layer of fat lime plaster, about half an inch thick. Over that, a coating consisting of a mixture of fine sand, marble powder, and gypsum to even out the surface. This is allowed to dry before finally adding a thin layer of calcined gypsum that will serve as the base for fixing the colors. This last coat is applied on the same day that the artist will begin to paint, after having dampened the preceding layer with a leaf-shaped trowel."

I must have coughed—the young man turns. He looks me over from head to foot and lets out an obnoxious little whistle. From the wine-colored mark on his forehead and cheeks—little Vito had described the birthmark to me—I know it must be Batisto, Tassi's assistant. He glances up at the scaffolding where, due to the darkness in the nave, I hadn't noticed his master, Agostino Tassi, the handsome conquistador with the black beard.

"Agostino, take a look at the little wonder that just appeared!"

Batisto continues to undress me with his eyes. "So, my pretty little thing, have you lost your mama?"

I stick my tongue out at him.

Tassi signals his assistant to leave me in peace. In his turn, he quietly contemplates me. I have no words to describe the emotions I see fleeting over his face. I think they frighten me.

I muster all of my courage. "Would you happen to know where I might find Master Gentileschi?"

"He isn't here," Tassi simply replies. Then he adds, still staring at me, "You might just well do for a model. But I would like to have a closer look at you."

Who does he think he is? We're not at the horse market! I try to find a quick answer. "Please don't bother. Is it not true that frescoes are to be admired from a distance?"

He laughs. "That is quite true indeed." Nevertheless he begins climbing down the tiers of rickety scaffolding.

"There's no need for you to come all the way down to observe me right under your nose. I only pose for my own paintings."

Tassi stops short. In a condescending tone that infuriates me, he says, "A young woman who can draw? How wonderful! And above all, how bold of you to try to paint yourself . . ." After a short silence he adds, "It's a hopeless endeavor!"

My indignation and surprise must have flashed in my eyes. Tassi is pleased with the effect he has obtained. He smiles kindly at me. "Who could be talented enough to render such magnificent beauty?"

He is definitely making fun of me! It is easy to see he's very accustomed to dealing with women. I shut up like an oyster, throw my drawings on the floor and snap dryly, "Be so kind as to tell Master Gentileschi that I have finished the sketches."

As I am stomping furiously over to the door, Tassi asks, "And who shall I tell him called, if you please?"

I wish I could turn around and get one last look at the finely shaped, smirking mouth that uttered this last sentence, but I resist the temptation. Without turning, and in a voice that I pray sounds utterly confident, I respond, "His daughter."

14

We're all sitting around the long kitchen table, as we do every Sunday. Today, my father broached a small cask of wine and slit the throats of three chickens, accomplishing his act of violence for the week.

The assistants are wolfing down the meal and joking loudly, while Tuzia and the young maid serve. Marco is playing with the cat under the table. I'm just sitting very still, staring glassy-eyed at my untouched plate, lost in daydreams. It irritates me to have all these uncontrollable thoughts—desires?—crowding in on me. It is almost obscene.

What could I have said to Tassi to take the wind out of his sails?

I'd like to snip off that pitch-black beard he seems so proud of! Why had he looked at me in that way? Why had so many unspoken things passed between us, the meaning of which he alone seemed to understand? We had communicated in a way that was beyond words, and the warm bubble in my womb had something to do with it. What am I talking about? I don't understand any of it. In reality, the only thing that interests me about the man is that he paints out-of-doors, and he is an expert in perspective, that is the extent of it. I might also add that his coming to our little village did liven things up a little. Nothing more.

How long can I go on fooling myself?

For one whole week I remain closed to the world, quiet and pensive, like a rock that Tassi is washing over and submerging at regular intervals.

I keep finding myself dawdling aimlessly about my father's studio, not speaking to anyone, my mind in a whirl, impervious to everything. Except the mention of Tassi. When any of the assistants happen to utter his name, it's as if a shimmering cloud comes floating over to me and explodes like fireworks in my head. Thus, here and there, I glean snatches of the distant existence the adventurer leads and, for a few instants, have the impression of living by his side.

It makes me furious to realize how much influence this complete stranger has over me.

Young Vito, who wishes to retain his status of spy, or who is simply a lot smarter than I think, comes to see me in my tent. He looks at my most recent drawings, for—despite my errant ways—I haven't stopped working.

"Doesn't your Saint Luke happen to have a remarkable resemblance to Agostino Tassi?" Since Vito is always bright-eyed, it's impossible to tell whether it is an innocent question or if he has discovered my secret.

"Do you really think so? I don't at all."

The child begins to recount the latest anecdotes from around the work site, where he now spends the greater part of his time. According to him, Tassi and my father are thick as thieves now. Tassi is the protégé of Cosimo Quorli, the Pope's friend and secretary. Quorli comes to see him often. Tassi has half of the girls in the region posing for him; it has gotten to the point that one literally bumps into naked women in the church.

"It's fun, very bouncy!" the boy affirms.

Tassi this, Tassi that . . . It seems that Vito absolutely worships the artist.

"And he's strong as an ox! Do you know what he did yesterday?"

I interrupt him with a shrug. "I couldn't care a whit about your Tassi. Can't you keep quiet for a minute? Here, take a needle and help me punch holes in this cartoon.

I observe Vito secretly: The dark wisps of his curls, the high cheekbones, his delicate, impertinent nose, those full, sensual lips, but above all his eyes, long slanted eyes like those of a Moor, fringed with thick black lashes. Tassi must have looked like Vito when he was a child.

The sun went down quite a while ago. Vito is nodding over his work, he can barely keep his eyes open. I gather him up in my arms, the contact of my skin against his makes him fall asleep almost instantly. He is much lighter than my brother Marco, who is nevertheless much younger. This child is undernourished, and ill-treated as well, by Roberto and the other assistants. Most important of all, the boy lacks love and affection.

I carry my sleepy little bundle down the gravel path, being very careful not to trip, and enter the dark studio. Slowly, following the even sounds of deep breathing, I make my way over to the corner where the apprentices sleep, lay Vito down on the rough pallet, roll my turban up under his head, and pull the blanket over his frail shoulders.

As I kiss his forehead near the hairline, he murmurs, "Mama . . . ," just like a baby.

I force back the burning tears that rush to my eyes and swear by all that is sacred to protect this child from now on. He isn't as lucky as Marco, for, despite the aversion I feel for her, I must admit that Tuzia is a fair mother to my brother. Whereas for Vito, I promise myself that one day I will make him my assistant.

How long have I been sitting on the garden wall? My rump is as hard and cold as stone. I'm getting all stiff, and yet I haven't the slightest desire to go to bed.

Tonight, the moon is full, it gazes down upon me with its pale round eye. The full moon has always deeply affected me.

The moon that pulls back the tides, exposing crabs, unwary fish, smooth round shingles, the whole deepsea world, has a similar effect on me. It feels as though the familiar part of me is drawn far away, baring the hidden side of my being.

It is a different Artemisia, a phantom in a white nightgown, who suddenly stands and walks resolutely toward the dunes.

The white house on the beach seems to glitter in the pearly light of the moon. Surely Tassi has been asleep for some time. Is his room on the ground floor? Upstairs? I can't imagine him wearing a nightcap as my father does. Does he sleep in the nude? I picture the sheet thrown back, with one corner of it trapped between his muscular thighs . . .

In spite of the din made by the waves, just as I am nearing the house I believe I can hear the sound of a lute.

Sighs, loud voices now mingle with the notes of music. I stealthily skirt the terrace and sneak along the wall backed by the dunes. Light is pouring out of two windows up ahead of me.

I pull myself up onto my tiptoes and stifle a nervous laugh. That day at the creek, I thought I had learned everything there was to know about what men and women do together. But I was a long way from imagining anything like this!

Looking through the frame of the windowpane, I can see around twenty people, men and women, crowded onto various mattresses, some lying on the bare floor. The bodies are knotted together in clusters of two, three, even four, in positions that are so complex, I could never have conceived of them.

Directly in front of me, on the large wooden bed that is reminiscent of a Spanish galleon with the figure of a sea nymph proudly adorning its bow, Batisto and another assistant are laboring over a woman. I don't really understand. Have they both penetrated her by the same cavity or are they taking her through two different orifices? In any case, the exercise is turning Batisto such a vivid shade of crimson that his birthmark almost fades in with the rest of his skin.

With a graceful twist, he extricates himself, grabs a piece of paper,

and quickly begins to sketch a couple fornicating. Several similar drawings are scattered about at his feet. He'll get a good price for them. I've
heard that pornography sells well in Rome.

A myriad of candles light up the vast room. To my great surprise, I
notice Cosimo Quorli, the secretary to the Pope, sprawled out on a
mountain of cushions like an obscene Pantagruel. He is not indulging
in the debauchery. With his yellow velvet vest buttoned up to the col-
lar, one hand stuck down the front of his trousers, he is popping grapes
into his mouth as he avidly observes the scene being enacted at his feet—
shod with gold-buckled slippers. Two buxom young women lying head
to toe, are lustfully licking and petting each other.

Was this friendly little party thrown in his honor? Why not? Even
though I wasn't expecting it, I know that Quorli has a reputation for
being licentious. In any case, there's no denying that Agostino Tassi
bends over backward to please his patrons! Perhaps Batisto's drawings
were also intended for the man from the Vatican. A way of offering him
a lasting souvenir from this charming get-together.

I'm trying to act nonchalant, very worldly-wise, but in truth, I'm
quite unnerved. Especially when Tassi himself suddenly appears within
my range of vision.

He teeters over toward Cosimo Quorli, his shirt half unbuttoned, a
glass of wine in his hand. His disheveled state becomes him.

The corpulent Quorli calls out to him, as his pudgy, ring-laden fingers fondle the buttocks gyrating within his reach. "Don't drink so
much, Agostino! If you're drinking because you're worried about your
future, you have no need to be. As long as the Pope has confidence in
me, you will be commissioned by God's clients themselves."

Tassi winks at him and walks unsteadily away.

He can't just up and disappear like that. I creep along the wall to the
next window.

It looks into a kind of private sitting room, very scantily furnished.
Agostino is standing there alone, nimbused in the soft glow of the can-

dles. A drop of wine has left a stain on his shirtfront, just over the heart, and the wan light of the moon lends a sickly pallor to his face. He looks as if he's been wounded in battle. I find him just sublime.

The beautiful vision is suddenly cut short.

A naked woman with enormous breasts walks up and rubs herself against Tassi. She clings to him, covers his chest with kisses, moves down lower, unlaces his trousers, pushes her mouth smeared with an outrageous color of red between his legs . . . Tassi's eyes close with pleasure.

I want to scream.

In my discomfiture, I must have bumped my forehead against the window. Having heard the noise, Agostino turns toward me. Our eyes meet, lock desperately together, like two people drowning.

Tassi pushes the woman away abruptly and rushes to the window . . . I'm already long gone.

15

I don't recall how I made it back to my room, how it happened that my heart thudding so wildly in my chest did not awaken the whole house, or how my feet remembered of their own accord to avoid the fifth step, the one that creaks so loudly.

I'm in pain, terrible pain. Until today, I only knew of the existence of physical pain. I'm totally disoriented. I almost feel as though I'll lose my balance. I fling open the window, the cool air soothes me a bit. I look at the tall pine tree in the garden and I wish I could climb up to the very top of it and jump off. I imagine what the fall would be like, broken ever so slightly by the supple branches. No, I don't want to die, I just want the pain in my soul to be transformed into bodily suffering.

So, I fall back on the only remedy I know of, drawing. As always, when the meaning of things eludes me, I commit my feelings of uncertainty to paper. It's my way of refusing to be submissive, of acting, of forcing a turn of events by re-creating them on paper, from my point of view.

Twenty times over, I reproduce the scene that has so upset me; twenty times, I revive that rictus of pleasure on Tassi's face that the mouth of the creature sucking his phallus provoked. My angry fingers race over the paper. It's obvious that he doesn't love that woman. He might hardly even know her. Why would he allow himself to be seduced in that way? What makes her so alluring? She seemed hideous to me. I find it rather humiliating to consider the ugliness of my rival a victory, but that's the way I feel, I can't help it. Now, I even begin to accentuate her defects in my sketches. I embellish her unfortunate looks, giving her a hook nose, a toothless, wrinkled-up mouth, and bulging, froglike eyes.

It's that I've just noticed, in the first drawings, instead of that witch's face, I had drawn my own.

16

Taking on the apprentice's chores is a welcome change for me. My mind was in a turmoil when I awoke this morning. "Go out and play on the beach," I had said to Vito, "and pass me that wide paintbrush."

I lean over and begin energetically swabbing a coat of gesso over the new canvas when suddenly someone kicks me in the rear end. The shock flings me to the floor and a voice orders, "Run and fetch your master, son!"

I whirl around with a vengeance that sends my turban flying, and my hair comes tumbling down in a cascade of curls. Tassi is standing over me, gazing at me in shocked mortification. "Pardon me! I took you for a student . . ."

Now it is my turn to be embarrassed. Wiping off my gesso-smeared cheeks with the back of my hand, I furtively straighten my tangled hair. I shouldn't have done that. Nothing escapes this man. He will think that I'm playing the coquette with him.

Tassi politely offers his hand to help me up. I decline, jump quickly to my feet, and snarl, "Oh really? You thought I was a student? So that is the way you're accustomed to treating your apprentices?"

Knowing I must be red-faced with humiliation, I can only hope that he will think it is outrage.

Speaking of colors, Tassi is dressed entirely in black, and it becomes him very well. He remains standing there in front of me with a bemused smile on his face. "The first time I saw you, I thought you were a model. Today, I took you for a boy." His voice grows lower, takes on gentle, slightly teasing inflections, "And yesterday, perhaps for a phantom at my window . . ."

I look down, unable to meet his eyes. "But I forgive you," he adds, "if you'll forgive this unfortunate kick in the pants."

There is a moment of awkward silence. Quick, we must change the subject.

Tassi takes the initiative. "Very well! Let me see one of your pieces, Miss Chameleon!"

I start, and suddenly I'm elated. Really, I wasn't expecting this in the least.

"Come, I'll show you my studio," I say enthusiastically.

He seems taken aback. "Your studio?"

As I lead the way, I think about how erratic my emotions are. Is it because of my youth? My inexperience? Only a moment ago, I was trembling before the man that I've become obsessed with. The man who mysteriously causes the bubble within me to throb. Now, I feel like a novice in whom a great master has shown interest. Or pretends to show interest in. I am suddenly stricken with doubt. Could Tassi be making fun of me? It's not the impression I get. On the contrary, he seems charmed with my improvised studio. Impatient to learn his opinion, I brandish the small self-portrait at him rather than simply showing it calmly. You must temper your enthusiasm, Artemisia, try not to appear to be so passionate.

Tassi contemplates my painting for a long time before comparing it with my anxious face. "This is your father's work."

With an indignant shudder I reply, "No it's not, it's my work. That is my face and I painted it myself."

Am I dreaming, or does he really seem to be impressed?

Orazio enters the tent, cutting my thoughts short. "Ah, Agostino, here you are! Artemisia has lured you into her den."

My father casts a stern look at me, as if to scold me for bothering Tassi.

I decide to take the defensive, "He's the one who asked to see my work!"

Orazio ignores my response and leads his associate away by the arm. "I'm taking you to dinner at the inn."

Papa made me look ridiculous, he humiliated me. Did he do it on purpose?

17

Sleep came suddenly.

All of my dreams revolved around painting. I visited churches that don't exist, encountered Michelangelo, took a lesson in anatomy from Mantegna, conversed with Botticelli, observed the flight of birds in the company of Leonardo da Vinci.

Not the slightest sign of Tassi.

I even imagined myself working on paintings. Above all, a *Judith and Holofernes,* that I remember distinctly and that I fully intend to actually render one day. It was partly inspired by the Caravaggio piece I had so admired at the Academy in Rome. Except that, whereas the Neapolitan master's Judith was cutting off a resigned head with no less ease than grace, mine—much more resolute—was viciously decapitating a struggling body, with blood splattered everywhere. I wanted the onlooker to feel the bones resisting under the steel blade.

A fragment of conversation slipped into my dreams, breaking up the order. I opened my eyes; it was still dark. The voices were coming from downstairs, in the kitchen. My father's deep voice and that of my stepmother with its whiny notes. They spoke my name: that's enough to make me leave my bed, go over to the top of the stairs, and sit down to listen quietly to what is being said.

What a pity that I missed the beginning. I picture them sitting with their elbows on the greasy wooden table, their nightcaps pulled down over their ears, and their nightshirts not long enough to cover their bare feet. Tuzia is always complaining about having cold feet.

I can only hear snatches of the sentences. "She never listens to anything. All she ever thinks about is drawing," Tuzia says at one point.

My father sounds irritated. "It was just an idea . . . I haven't even mentioned it to her yet."

"It's a husband that she needs," carps Tuzia, "not a teacher."

Now this is getting interesting. Interesting enough for me to venture down a few more steps. A teacher? And where was such a teacher to be found? I already have Papa, but I have nothing against the idea of learning from someone else, and Orazio seems to feel the same way.

"I don't have much left to teach her. And the whole studio would benefit from it. We need new ideas, my inspiration is running thin."

Tuzia interrupts him dryly, "I'm against it. It's unsuitable for a young woman. Perhaps, if she could study under a woman, I would consider it, but there's no such thing as a woman painter."

A chair scrapes on the floor. My father leaves the table with these words: "Artemisia is my daughter! I won't have you interfering in her future."

Well said! Thank you, Papa. I can almost forgive him for having deprived me of Tassi's company yesterday. But not quite . . .

18

I have given careful thought to this idea of a teacher.

Although I can almost trace all of the letters in the alphabet, I do not yet know how to write. Nevertheless, in theory, my crayon should be able to represent words as easily as it can create forms on paper.

So I have "written" out a list in three columns.

In the first column, I note down the artistic skills I have already perfected. Those that I would like to acquire—perspective and painting from nature, among other things—are listed in the second column. Finally, the third column is comprised of everything that I do not want to learn, and that I will never allow any teacher to inculcate me with. It is more a question of morals or professional ethics than of technique. I do not wish to have my personal character squelched and become like all those painters who endlessly repeat the tired methods developed by their elders, nor do I intend to submit, as is customary, to the whims of clients who know nothing about art, who judge a painting by how well it goes with the the decor of a sitting room or the color of the walls. How many times have I heard my father's clients say something like, "Paint me a handsome martyr with Roman arenas in the background. It will go well with the stone lions in my dining room."

As a result, I've come to the decision that my objective is to remain forever free, and to evolve. I am therefore in need of a professor who will care for me as I do the almond tree in our garden.

When we first moved here, I immediately noticed that tree. I take care of it every day. I give it just the right amount of water, never too much. I speak to it as I would a friend and scold it as I would a child, whenever it allows itself to be overrun with parasites.

Above all, I make sure that the stakes I planted around its still slender trunk do not stunt its growth, but allow it instead to take on a unique form. The trunk will bend in the manner that I have decided, but I will leave its branches free to grow as they will. I am simply helping it to grow tall. One day, I'll stop intervening, and everyone will admire its originality.

Where can I find a teacher, a gifted gardener of this sort?

Actually, I've known the answer from the very beginning.

I choose several drawings from those my father had rejected, and put aside most of the others I had carried in the green portfolio on the day I went to the Academy. This is not what I should show Agostino! I'd rather play for higher stakes, wager all or nothing. If I'm not mistaken about him, if he truly is the teacher I am looking for, then he must see what I hide from everyone else.

I lift the floorboard under which my most secret drawings are hidden, the nudes of Fulvio in the cave as well as the studies of my own body. There are also a few bizarre essays at transcribing my nocturnal dreams and some exercises of a very personal nature. As for the sketches I made from my recollections of what I saw that night in the house on the beach, I burned them all.

Today I'm in no hurry to reach Monte Cavallo's church; I am in such a good mood that I play at balancing my portfolio on my head as I walk along. I hum a pretty tune and do a little jig, I even pick a sunflower. As I've seen lovesick girls do, I pluck off the petals one by one chanting, "He'll love to be my teacher, he won't love to be my teacher . . ." The last petal ends with, "He'll love to be my teacher," which is a good sign.

Vito is setting the bowls of bean soup down in front of the apprentices who are sitting around a makeshift table. Tassi is not among them. All the better. That means he's inside the church and I'll be able to be alone with him. I slip in through the small door at the back so that no one will see me.

Agostino is standing under the scaffolding, vigorously scrubbing at the paint stains on his hands and arms with a piece of cloth. My handsome adventurer—I mean to say my respected teacher—doesn't wear an artist's smock. I can't help but admire his bare back, muscular and lithe at the same time. His stomach bulges slightly, not from fat, but as if pushed forward by the abdominal wall. There are sparse white hairs on his torso. His chest is prominent, somewhat feminine; it stirs me, makes me flush.

Get a hold of yourself, Artemisia, you must be a serious student. Just go up to him and explain everything. No, not everything . . .

I cough slightly to get his attention and hold out my portfolio. "Please take me as your student. You must! I have nothing more to learn from my father, and the Academy refuses to accept me."

That was terrible, Artemisia! You should have wished him good day first, struck up a polite conversation, introduced the subject adroitly . . .

Agostino doesn't seem surprised to see me, which irritates me a little. He calmly finishes wiping his hands before opening the green portfolio. He studies my drawings in silence, one after the other. Twisting a mesh of hair, I nervously await the verdict. Tassi skims quickly over the anatomical studies that I did from my own body, as though they were of little importance. So he's humiliating me once again!

The sketches of Fulvio's body bring him up short and his eyes fix mine. Am I imagining things, or is there a hint of jealousy in that look?

"I don't suppose you showed these to the director of the Academy."

"No."

"Or to your father."

I shake my head.

"And you've decided to share your secrets with with me?"

I blush. An embarrassing silence falls and seems to draw out interminably. "Are you asking me to become your professor, or your confessor? No, no, dealing with one Gentileschi is already complicated enough. I simply cannot. I'm not interested."

Agostino closes the green portfolio. I refuse to believe it. The gardener is brushing me aside, as if I were a useless weed!

"One day, I'll paint circles around you. Then it will be you who'll be asking to study under me!" I manage to blurt before running out the door.

With tears streaming from my eyes, I race blindly from the church. I only know that I'm not running in the direction of home. I cross the pine forest and head out toward the marshland. I'll never go home again. I wish I were dead. I am dead already, crushed with bitter disappointment and humiliation.

The low branches lash at my face, the thistles tear into the skin on my ankles; it seems as if all the birds in the world are mockingly singing my defeat.

Through blurred eyes, I vaguely make out a silhouette up in front of me, standing between two trees. Tomasso, the woodsman? No, he's much taller than that. Who could it be then? I don't want to find out and veer off to one side. In any case, I don't want to speak with anyone today.

The form blocks my path of escape. The pine forest is filled with the smell of an expensive perfume, and I feel a fat little hand grab hold of my wrist. Something gleams on the hand; the fingers are covered with rings. I can neither make out the features of the face, nor the lips that are pronouncing my name.

"Oh-ho! Artemisia, the young lady painter . . ."

I wipe the tears away with the back of my hand. Now I can see clearly.

"Don't be afraid," he says, loosening his grip on my wrist. "Allow me to introduce myself, Cosimo Quoril, secretary to the Pope."

Yes, I recognized you! All right, now I hope you'll leave me in peace now. I really have no desire to converse with anyone. I just want to be alone.

Cosimo suddenly pulls me toward him. He is panting in short, uneven breaths against my cheek. It isn't a good sign. His voice takes on a vulgar slur: "So, did you enjoy our little evening at Tassi's? I saw you looking in the window, you know. Come over here now, you little wench."

All of a sudden, fear overwhelms me. I have never felt this kind of terror before. I try to wriggle free, but Quorli's hold on me is rock solid. "Keep still, you dirty whore. I'll give you a closer look at what a man is. It's useless to fight, I tell you!"

Quorli throws me brutally to the ground and flings himself on top of me. He stuffs a handful of pine needles in my mouth to stifle my cries, pins me down with his knees as he unfastens his fly with one hand, spreads my legs, and searches the folds of my dress to find my flesh with the other. A small, purplish member rises over the swell of my pubescence. The eyes of the Pope's secretary seem to shrink with lustful desire while mine grow wide with horror. The bubble in my abdomen knows that he'll penetrate me any second, and it is screaming that it doesn't want this, that I must do something quickly . . . I bring my knee up hard into his testicles, spitting the pine needles out in his face.

My assailant screams and doubles over in pain. I gather my portfolio up hastily and take off at a dead run. Some of the nude sketches I'd done of my body slip from the folder and scatter in the wind. My first instinct is to run after them, but I decide against it for lack of time, but also because I tell myself that if the infamous Quorli is a souvenir collector, he can at least take these home with him.

19

"Artemisia," scolds my stepmother, "stop wasting water. The well is almost dry!"

Soaking wet, draped in a coarse bath cloth, gripping with both hands the handle of a bucket that is so full it is slopping water at each step, I silently struggle past Tuzia, busy with her washing. Off in one corner, Marco is playing Prince Valiant, with a paper helmet over his face and wooden sword in hand, in combat with an invisible enemy. He throws himself down on one knee in front of me, putting his hand to his heart, and proclaims emphatically, "Gentle maiden, hasten to the wellhead and draw the water to freshen your beauty for your young squire."

Would that you knew the truth, young brother, you would take up your sword and hasten to cleave in twain the scoundrel who wished harm upon your sister.

I don't know how many times I've walked back and forth to the well. My skin is burning from scrubbing it with the haircloth and strong soft soap. My hair has the texture of rope from being lathered and rinsed so much. I even washed out the inside of my mouth with a mixture of mint leaves and ground charcoal, but nothing does any good. The feeling of defilement is indelible.

I massage the bruised flesh of my thighs, my shoulders, my wrists, in hopes of erasing the finger marks left by the Pope's secretary. The blood refuses to return to the white mottled blotches. From white, they turn a deep red, then purple. Until they disappear—which will take some time—I will have to learn live with them. Just the sight of them makes me nauseous, makes me constantly relive the terrible experience in my mind. I am haunted by the horrid grimace that deformed the rapist's face, I can still feel the touch of his sweaty hands on my skin, I can hear his shallow breathing, and can see the aggressive erect organ with which he meant to spear me.

After having escaped the clutches of Cosimo Quorli, I ran straight home in spite of the fact that I'd vowed never to return after Tassi had refused me. I was afraid that everyone in the studio would learn about my vain attempt and make fun of me. But this ignoble encounter has changed my childish decision. I needed someplace to take refuge. What more secure a shelter than a father's house? When, as I rounded a corner and caught sight of the friendly facade, and heard the echoes of familiar voices, I let out a sigh of gratitude, and thought to myself, "Nothing has changed!"

How sadly mistaken I was, how utterly wrong! Now I will have to grow accustomed to the idea that the young woman I once was has been reduced to nothing, has gone up in smoke like a piece of straw thrown onto a roaring blaze. Offered up to the fires of hell. Cosimo Quorli did not ravish my virgin body, but he violated my chaste heart. Gone is the candor, the innocence, and all of those fine illusions about love!

The first thing I learned about love was the way that animals copulate, which always struck me as a little comical. When we were children, Fulvio and I would laugh awkwardly as we watched them rutting and grunting after one another. Then there had been, successively, the lovers I'd spied on at the creek, the desire that I had felt budding in Fulvio, the mysterious feelings that Tassi inspires in me, and finally, that evening of debauchery that I had watched from the window. I was shocked by the excesses I witnessed there, but at least all of the participants seemed to be consenting. Up until this afternoon, I thought that the act of lovemaking only involved feelings of tenderness. Cosimo Quorli taught me about brutality, bestiality, horror, and repugnance, even worse: he taught me loathing for myself. Now I will know how to recognize men of that breed at a glance and avoid them at all costs.

In rummaging through my trunk trying to find a clean-smelling white dress, I think of all the friends I have seen go off on the arms of unknown husbands, ugly men, older than they, enticed by their youth, their beauty, but not in the least concerned with their soul. I myself was resigned to accept the same fate, someday. I used to tell myself, "It's the custom, one must certainly end up developing a certain fondness . . ."

Today I have decided once and for all that no one will ever impose a husband upon me. Now I know that sharing a bed with someone who inspires only instinctive aversion in one's heart is the worst thing that can happen to a woman. Moreover, I was able to fight against Quorli, refuse to submit, but when married . . .? Spread one's legs as a matter of duty whenever the other expresses the desire? Never.

I am beginning to feel a little better now. My almond tree, like a faithful friend, helps me to escape and look on the brighter side of things. I'm spending the evening scraping its trunk and branches to rid it of the parasites that were attacking it again. It's another way of pursuing the deep cleansing I have undertaken.

Marco is giving me a hand. My stepmother is hanging wash out on the line. Seeing us working at gardening, she shrugs. She thinks it ridiculous to spend so much time on a tree.

My little brother had begged me to help him find a promising young offshoot. "Your almond tree will be 'the big sister' and mine will be 'the little brother' just like in real life!"

The assistants are coming back from the site, singing one of the pretty local tunes. Of course, Roberto isn't singing, he's bringing up the rear, scowling as usual. Barely has he closed the door of the studio after himself when my brother exclaims, picking over the bark as if it were a head of hair, "I'd wager there are more lice than this on Roberto's head!"

Papa comes in through the gate and walks directly over to me. "What have you gone and said to Tassi, Artemisia? He tells me you have been causing disturbances."

That's just what I was afraid of, the man is impossible. He's up and told everyone what I said and probably twisted everything as well! Livid with shame, I answer, "I told him nothing but the truth. That I can paint well enough to become his student."

"Misia! You will have to be more amiable with him . . ."

Amiable? I'd rather be buried alive! To think that I used to call him my adventurer . . .

A wry smile breaks out on my father's face. "Especially since I convinced him to give you lessons three times a week."

What? The handsome adventurer consented? I throw my arms around Papa's neck, smother him with kisses, and let my apron and scraping tool drop to the ground.

"Where are you going?" asks my father.

Prancing around impatiently, I manage to blurt, "To my lesson!"

Orazio takes hold of my arm. "Stop acting like a child, Misia. Painting lessons are not given at night. Do you think that you'll be able to wait until tomorrow?"

"And, since it is out of the question that you go alone," Tuzia adds, "I'll accompany you tomorrow. After I've finished the housework, of course."

Then one might as well say never! My stepmother can always find something to polish or scrub. And anyway, I don't want to be burdened with that shrew!

Luckily Papa comes to my rescue. "No, Tuzia! Someone needs to stay home while I'm working at the site. We can send Marisa . . ."

Our little maid-turned-chaperone, that suits me just fine. She is self-effacing, gentle, obedient, and a bit of a dunce. She won't hamper with me much.

20

I am up and ready to go to my lesson before the rooster has stopped crowing. I have a hard time deciding whether to wear my artist's garb, or a dress. I choose the everyday green dress, with very little corseting, that allows for freedom of movement. If I need to, I'll put an apron over it.

I wait as patiently as possible for the cock to crow a second time. There he goes, the reliable old fellow, letting his glorious carillon ring out! Tassi and his assistants will surely be awake now.

In the cubbyhole under the stairs that has been converted into a tiny bedroom, I find Marisa still sleeping soundly. Since she's been promoted to the status of chaperone, she probably thinks that she'll finally get the chance to sleep in a little later on the three days that I have my lesson. Isn't she just as eager as I am to climb to the top of the dunes, to feel the cool morning sand between her toes, to run toward the white house on the beach? What a loafer! I immediately regret having thought such a thing; the poor girl works all year round without a single day of rest. Up at the break of dawn, she empties the chamber pots, straightens the house, scrubs the floors, polishes and dusts, and finally flops onto her bed when the dinner dishes have been stacked up to dry.

My profuse and admirable compassion does not deter me from shaking her impatiently all the same.

Marisa is trotting along behind me, stifling her yawns. She's having difficulty keeping up with me. I breast the dunes at a run and, once on the other side, have to refrain from letting myself roll down to the bottom of the slope as I so love to do. It wouldn't be appropriate for a new student to arrive at her lesson covered with sand.

Out in front of the white house, the assistants are busy with their morning ablutions. Naked to the waist, they are splashing themselves with cold water and laughing loudly. Our arrival excites them all the more. While one of the young men starts banging a bucket against the side of the well, the others welcome us with a concert of shrill whistles. Batisto, Tassi's senior assistant, begins to strut about like a turkey in mating season staring insolently at Marisa. I chuckle inwardly, thinking that the red birthmark on his face actually does make him look like a plump barnyard fowl.

The racket is such that it brings Tassi hurrying out. He is so tall that he must stoop to go through the door.

Agostino has shaved off part of his beard, only a goatee remains. Now, more than ever, he resembles a legendary conquistador. Yet, with his handsome face still creased with sleep, there is something fragile about him, he seems more accessible. His shirt is buttoned wrong, he has one boot on and is holding the other in his hand. A sudden wave of fondness for him swells within me.

He stops in the doorway, crosses his arms, and upbraids the young men in a hoarse voice. "Now I won't put up this ruckus every day, I tell you! This is my new student, Artemisia. She'll be studying with us on Mondays, Wednesdays, and Fridays. Show her what nice young men you are and greet her courteously with words of welcome."

Coming from all sides at once, I am submerged by a hearty chorus of "Good morning, signorina," followed by exaggeratedly low bows. It occurs to me that, unlike my father, who will not tolerate impertinence or promiscuity under his roof, Tassi represents more of a big brother for his assistants than a master. In any case, Orazio would never organize an orgy to entertain his assistants!

Agostino motions for us to come a little closer.

"There's nothing to be afraid of. They won't bite you."

I'm not as much of a sissy as he thinks. Am I not just as used to being surrounded by men as he is? Intimidated all the same, the only reply that comes to mind is, "They don't frighten me."

Tassi glances at Marisa. "I see that you've come with your own apprentice in tow," he says. "Does everyone think that I've opened a school?"

It's clear to me that the real meaning behind these words is, "So, they've gone and saddled you with a nursemaid!"

Intrigued, Marisa reaches out to touch the scale model of a ship set on a stand and leaning up against the house. I catch her by the waistband of her skirt and shake her gently, "Let's keep our hands to ourselves, Marisa!"

Batisto seems to see things differently. A raffish glint lights his eyes and, taking a provocative stance, his pelvis thrust forward indecently, he sneers, "Oh no, you can handle things as much as you like!"

The joke makes all of the apprentices laugh. Losing his patience, Agostino leads Marisa away by the arm. "Young ladies, I believe it would be best if we were to work at a safe distance from these ruffians. We'll meet with less distractions in a quieter setting."

We enter the large room on the ground floor that is used as a studio. Not a sign of the sexual abandon that had taken place here, what meets the eye is a room intended for work. Just as in my father's studio, there are easels everywhere, piles of blank canvases, reams of drawing and tracing paper. In the middle of the room, set out on a small pedestal, a wooden figurine catches my eye. I've never seen anything like it, it is the size of an adult male and is perfectly proportioned, the head is faceless, smooth as an egg. It must have been stuck away in some cupboard on that infamous night, or else, being too fascinated with the lechery, I hadn't noticed it from the window where I was posted. Tassi explains to me how the joints work and I play at putting the mannequin into absurd postures.

The bed still waits on the platform, its prow representing the naked torso of a sea nymph with generous breasts. Perturbed, Marisa asks in an uncomfortable whisper, "Do you really think it is his bed?"

She spoke too loudly. Agostino bursts out laughing. "Of course not. It's simply one of the props."

He darts a look in my direction that is so heavy with meaning, it makes me blush. When I close my eyes, the scene of that night comes back to me and almost seems more precise. Men and women intertangled, twisted bodies, enlacing one another in the golden light of the torches, and that creature pushing her painted lips between the legs of my bold adventurer. . . . I open my eyes with a start. Marisa is standing near Tassi. Too near. I nonchalantly nudge her aside and worm my way between them. The air around Agostino is warmer, laden with a reassuring, masculine scent that I breathe in through my nose in short little whiffs so as to better savor it. I wish I could always breathe this same air.

We begin with a still life—two pears, a pumpkin, and a lute arranged on a table. Sitting before an easel with my crayon lifted, I find it difficult to concentrate. Not only do I know nothing about still lifes, but also, I keep imagining that the lute I am supposed to reproduce on my paper is mysteriously playing the same tune as the other night.

Agostino's presence obsesses me. He's standing right behind me, which doesn't help matters either. The warmth emanating from his body makes my head reel and troubles me more than I would like. Also, although Marisa is keeping out of the way and pretending to ignore us, she never takes her eyes off me. She'd better not start taking her new role too seriously!

My pumpkin looks rather like an orange and my pears like lemons. Several times Tassi leaned over, putting his hands on my shoulders to examine the sketch. The contact of his palms still radiates through my body, my neck prickles deliciously where the soft beard brushed against it. And now his breath is stirring a wisp of my hair. I honestly would like to focus on the exercise. . . . How can I divorce myself from my feelings?

I can feel Agostino's slow hot gaze moving over my brow, down the back of my neck, along my bare arms and my hands. Is it an illusion?

"I'm sorry," I say to him, "I just can't seem to draw when you're watching me."

I rub out the whole neck of the lute once again, but Agostino pulls the crayon out of my hand. "Don't worry. It's never easy the first time. Pack up your things, we're going to try something else."

90

We leave Marisa behind, sleeping like a log, and walk out of the house. Tassi heads toward the beach. I follow, wondering what he has in mind. Finally he points to the hull of an abandoned boat.

"What do you see out there?"

The question stuns me, "A boat," I answer.

"But what else?"

"I don't know. Boats have never really inspired me."

"Try a little harder."

"I can't draw from nature. When there is no figure in the composition, it's as if I'm simply representing emptiness. And to tell you the truth, I've never seen anything as ugly as that boat of yours. It looks like the skeleton of a whale lying on its side."

"That's a little better. At least you've seen something. Come now, let's give it a try."

Brushing aside some dry seaweed, I sit down on the sand with my portfolio on my knees. Seated in this position, my dress rides up and reveals my calves. It embarrasses me. Tuzia always says that allowing anything to show above the ankles is indecent. I couldn't care less what my stepmother thinks. Even so, I tuck my legs over to one side and cover them as best I can. The position is very uncomfortable, but I never do feel very relaxed with Tassi anyway.

I trace a wobbly shape that very vaguely resembles the boat. To be more accurate, the first sketch looks like any old boat in the world. It lacks personality, is entirely lifeless, academic.

Tassi points out dryly, "You don't know how to observe things. Try again!"

My pride is stung. I insist on trying to improve on what I've already begun. Agostino rips the paper out of my hands and tears it to shreds.

"It's no good, I tell you. Look at things the way they truly are, with fresh eyes! You've painted portraits before, people don't all look alike, you depict their differences. I want a portrait of that boat."

I am feeling so peeved that I can barely keep my lips from trembling. I want to cry. This isn't how I imagined our first lesson to be. I had visions of my adventurer being enraptured by my artistic mastery, filled with mute admiration for the child prodigy, and here he is demanding that I perform impossible feats, pushing me headlong into unfamiliar territory. I stammer out lamely, "There's too much light out here. I'm not used to it . . ."

"Used to what? You came here to learn, didn't you?"

Yes of course, how right he is! He is the gardener I had dreamed of after all. The person who will see to it that I stick to the precept that is at the very top of my list: "Ever onward and upward!"

I drew the boat five times. Tassi tore the sketch up five times. Either it was the lichen and seaweed stuck to the hull that I had overlooked, or I hadn't adequately rendered the dilapidation of the loose, wind-worn boards, or else I was unable to reproduce the sharp shadows cast by the noonday sun.

As I become more disoriented, my hands fumble, are no longer sure of themselves; it seems to me that my drawing is getting worse by the minute. A woman's voice pulls me out of my quandary: someone is calling out the name of my handsome adventurer.

"Agostino! Agostino!"

I turn, intrigued by the tone of familiarity in the voice and can distinguish, against the light, the silhouettes of two men carrying a round-topped trunk and a third, more slender form, whose dress molds a staggeringly beautiful figure. Who is she? I'm burning to ask Tassi.

"The lesson is finished for today," my master says in a bland voice. Then he turns and strides off toward the woman who is calling him.

He leaves me sitting there alone in front of the boat.

A bitter flood of jealousy suddenly washes over me. It is even more intense than what I felt on the night the creature had been clinging to Tassi. Who is that woman? His mistress, his wife, perhaps? What is the meaning of that trunk? The intruder is moving into the white house, that much is obvious! Tears come streaming into my eyes, my heels beat angrily at the sand.

2 1

If that woman actually is Tassi's mistress, I'll have to find myself a new professor. I just wouldn't be able to stand running into her at each of my lessons.

I can't bring myself to ask Marisa what happened back in the big white house between Tassi and the woman. However, I find a million pretexts for broaching the subject, convinced that the young woman must know what I am alluding to. But my chaperone continues about her daily tasks as usual. Marisa is undoubtedly feeling quite important, wants to force me to ask her all sorts of questions. Unless she's simply not as sharp as I thought. Maybe it never even occurred to her that I had anything but a studious interest in Tassi.

Finally, not being able to stand it any longer, I ask indifferently, "That woman yesterday, do you think she's a student of Tassi's as well?"

"Oh no, not at all!"

"How can you be so sure?"

"They didn't notice me, or else they thought I was sleeping, or maybe they just didn't care. The lady's name is Costanza. She's very beautiful. It's easy to see she comes from the city! She immediately mentioned you, 'Who is that charming little thing?' Your teacher pretended not to have heard the question. He simply answered, 'You must have moved heaven and earth to find me here!' So then the woman said, 'Heaven? No, to be completely honest, heaven really never occurred to me at all.' And they both laughed. After that, she reproached him for having vanished like a thief in the night without even saying good-bye. He retorted, 'I thought we had nothing more to say to each other, but I see there is still one last thing left unsaid: Get out of my house!'"

Marisa stops to catch her breath as I am exulting.

"The woman didn't back down. She asked him to allow her to stay with him for just a little while. Master Tassi said, 'I don't love you anymore, you're well aware of that.' But the woman insisted, 'I don't care, I accept those terms and love you all the same.' She tried to take him into her arms and kiss him, but he pushed her away. To tell you the truth, I felt sorry for her."

Keep your feelings of pity to yourself, Marisa.

"The poor woman started begging him, swearing that she wouldn't be a bother, that she would do whatever he liked, that he needed a woman to look after the house, to prepare the meals for him and his apprentices, and so on. At one point she even said, 'You can pass me off as your sister, if you wish.' Tassi slapped his thigh, 'Ah, now that's an idea. Why not, after all? My sweet, loving sister!' and he smothered her with kisses."

Marisa stops for a moment, as if to collect the threads of her story. What happened next? What happened next? I'm dying to know.

"Oh, and then he called Batisto. The lady must have thought that he was going to have her thrown out because her eyes widened with fear. Batisto came running up, and Master Tassi said, 'I would like to introduce you to my sister, Costanza. Take good care of her. And don't hesitate to lavish upon her the type of affection that, without being morally offensive, a brother would bear for her.' You should have seen the woman's face!"

"And then?"

"Then that's all. As soon as they left the room, I came out to meet you."

Suddenly I feel very lighthearted. Right up to the very end, I had feared some sort of reversal. My sweet adventurer could have allowed his feelings of pity to get the better of him. I can hardly wait for the next lesson! From now on I will hate Tuesdays and Thursdays, the days that I won't see Agostino.

Although my conquistador has made me very unhappy on several occasions, and especially now that I know there is nothing between him and Costanza, I intend to be the most assiduous and docile of students. I want to surprise my master with my quick progress.

I therefore spend the rest of the afternoon scrutinizing the landscape. Squinting my eyes, I try to comprehend the mysteries of perspective. Oddly enough, I can fully grasp the idea of perspective with regard to the human body. Foreshortening an arm, depicting a leg as seen from a ground angle, a torso twisting backward, I can manage that. But as soon as I leave the studio, I become as awkward as if I had never held a crayon in my life. I'm barely able to actually observe the fact that the closer objects are to the horizon, the smaller they appear to be, or that distances are more blurred and bluish than foregrounds are.

How to go about reorganizing, on a flat surface, the immense chaos of nature? I discuss the matter with Papa, who admits he knows very little about the subject. "Landscape painting is something entirely new. It's too late for me to learn it now. But you, Misia, you belong to a new generation of painters. You should stay abreast of all the latest innovations. Tassi straddles the two schools. He will be able to train your eye, teach you the rules of painting from nature."

I almost feel like answering, "Yes, that and many other things as well . . ."

2 2

This morning Tassi is ready to begin the lesson when I arrive. His shirt is not buttoned incorrectly, nor is his face creased as it was the last time I saw him. He seems to have been up for some time and, under the long white smock, he's wearing his best clothing. I don't dare to think that he went to so much trouble just for me. He told Papa that I was nothing but a troublemaker. To be truthful, I must admit that he only agreed to become my professor out of friendship for my father.

With Marisa tagging along after us, we walk out to the edge of the beach where the blue line of the sea can be seen through the young pines and settle down in the shade. I am beginning to unpack my material when Tassi stops me. "No paper and crayon for the time being."

"What am I to draw with then?"

"With nothing but your eyes, in the same way as you told me you used to do at the convent."

Indicating the panorama that spreads before us with a sweep of his arm, he says, "Describe what you see to me."

"Rocks, sand, water, clouds . . ."

"You're not observing. Close your eyes!"

Has the man gone mad? Does he really believe that one can learn to paint by closing his eyes?

"Trust me. Go ahead . . ."

I resign myself and obey him with a sigh.

"The rocks," he begins, "form a compact mass, a sharp slanting line. First the mass curves slightly inward, then it bulges out like the brow of a child until it suddenly plunges into the yellow sand. Straight across from them, the narrow band of beach on the right seems almost to be a straight line, but that is an illusion. This line is also curved, dipping in, but much less deeply. Now, the sea, a grayish blue out at the horizon, it ripples and grows brighter with the passing currents, and when it dashes up against the beach or the rocks, it turns a deep emerald green, fringed with white foam."

Tassi's voice grows very soft, as if he were telling a bedtime story to a child. He describes each leaf, each stone, each shape, each color. Still keeping my eyes closed, I gradually let myself drift along with his words. "The sun," he continues, "is dancing out on the water. It makes a shimmering path that opens out at our feet no matter where we are standing. It's because we're facing it."

And he goes on for quite a long time, inventorying everything, describing it all in the most minute detail before he authorizes me to open my eyes. It's a revelation! My adventurer is a magician! He's changed my perception of the world. I discover the landscape as he described it with eyes that are much sharper, more sensitive to nuances, now able to discern the specific differences in each thing, to distinguish one from the other. My heart thrills in wonder: it's as if I'm seeing this beach for the very first time. Only one word comes to my lips, a word that encompasses all of the joy and amazement I feel: "Yes!"

But the lesson is not over yet. Agostino is now setting up the perspective frame. "I'll show you how to adjust it. It should always stand parallel to your body, perpendicular to the ground. This plumb line will be a great help to you. If the frame should lean forward, the proportions would no longer be respected, the view would flatten out. If it were leaning diagonally in relation to you, the view would appear elongated at the top."

I walk up to the wooden frame with reinforced corners. The metal wires strung between the struts divide the interior of the frame into equal squares, with sides approximately three digits in length.

"Like this?"

"Very good," Tassi says. "Now, stand the eyepiece around one and a half cubits from the frame, making sure that your eye is trained on the very center of the frame." He demonstrates for me, finishes adjusting the position of the instrument.

I close one eye and put the other up to the sight. "The wooden part of the instrument," he explains, "marks the limits of a picture frame, the area that the artists wishes to paint." He shows me how to use the apparatus. "Now, what do you see?"

"The world cut up into sections."

The squares formed by the cross wires indicate the correct position and the respective proportions for each of the elements in the landscape. That dune out there, half a square. The bushes over in the left corner, a whole square. The rock that looks like a dog sitting on its haunches, about one third of a square. I also notice that the line of the horizon cuts across the last line of squares; it looks awkward to me.

"Fine. Hoist the whole instrument up a little," Tassi suggests. "You need a bit more sky and less sea."

"That's better," I exclaim, after having followed his instructions.

"Notice how many distant things are contained in the squares at the top, in comparison with the few close-up objects that fit into the squares at the bottom. That is one of the effects of perspective."

An hour later, the instrument no longer holds much of a secret for me.

I'm very impatient to begin painting now. Tassi observes me as I rummage through the paintbrushes, choose the colors, arrange them on the palette. "Slow down, you can't start painting without sketching out the landscape first! For that matter, you could also put a figure in it if you like."

"Marisa will be perfect as a seashell gatherer!" I answer enthusiastically. "Marisa!"

My chaperone comes running up to us. Tassi takes her over to the hard wet sand left at low tide, and sets the pose. With one hand he makes her lean forward, and with the other he pulls her blouse down to reveal one shoulder. My cheeks burn at the sight of him touching her.

"How is that?" he cries, putting his hands up to his mouth like a megaphone.

"Ask her!" I shout back in aggravation.

Marisa is just standing there with a fatuous expression on her face. I'm just positive that she enjoys him fondling her like that, and also that Agostino has noticed my jealousy. It even amuses him, because he quickly takes his hands from Marisa's hips with a shrewd smile.

"Whatever can be wrong? I should think you would be pleased, we've come back to your cherished figures," he asks as he is walking back toward me.

With an irritated sigh I reply, "Even so, there's no need to spend all day setting the pose." I cast a mean look in poor Marisa's direction. "Marisa is only one element in the decor. I'm more interested in working with the color at this point!"

Tassi shakes his head, "But I have nothing to teach you about color."

"And why not? Aren't you supposed to teach me everything you know?"

"Of course, except that you know just as much as I do when it comes to color."

The compliment makes me blush right up to the very tips of my ears. "How mean of you not to have said that earlier, the one kind comment you had."

I look up into his eyes and find that he is contemplating me with surprising intensity. Could it be love I see?

Marisa pulls us out of our trance. "Do you want me to keep this pose?" she asks impatiently.

"Yes, that's fine," Agostino answers distractedly.

Embarrassed, I put my eye to the sight and begin my sketch.

My master devoted his whole day to me! We worked very hard and well, then we lunched on bread and cheese sitting in the shade of a tree.

It's late now, and Agostino is helping me pack up my material. I'm quite proud of my painting. For a first try it's not bad. Tassi points to the declining sun on the horizon. "The world around us is always new," he says, "and as we walk along, the horizon moves with us. Therefore, to give you an example, the sun sets earlier here than it does in Florence."

"So everyone sees a different sunset?"

My question makes him laugh. "Did you not know that the earth is round?"

I had always thought that the earth was flat, myself.

"You still have quite a few things to learn."

23

Nicolo, my father's agent, came by again today. Cosimo II, the grand duke of Tuscany would like to offer a representation of *Lucretia's Suicide* to his wife. Papa declines the offer with regret. "I can't accept any more work, Nicolo. You know full well that Monte Cavallo's church is taking all my time," he says.

"You could try to find some way to manage things differently."

"I can barely get by with the help of my assistants as it is," Orazio protests.

"An order from a Medici is not something one can easily refuse."

"Try to make the duke be a little more patient."

"One might just as well try to make the sun stop turning!"

"I'm sorry, Nicolo. The church frescoes must come first."

"You wouldn't have an old study of Cleopatra or another woman who committed suicide that could be changed into Lucretia?" Nicolo asks.

My father shakes his head regretfully. That is when I decide to pull him off to the side and beg him to entrust me with this project. Nicolo must know how to lip-read. He looks at me in astonishment and cries, "Another Gentileschi on the market! That crowns all! And how long have you been painting, young lady?"

Making him swear to keep the secret, Orazio confesses that the portrait of the man in armor could, to a great extent, be attributed to me. The agent is wide-eyed with disbelief. I show him my drawings; the small self-portrait he admires for a considerable time. And an avid glint begins to light his eyes.

"A woman painter, now there's something novel! Artemisia Gentileschi, the first woman painter in the history of art! The grand duke will love it! The discovery will have all of Italy seething with excitement."

He is obviously dreaming of all the gold he'll be making as well. Papa is frowning at him all the while. "Artemisia isn't yet prepared to take on such an important order."

I am stupefied; now it is the agent who must argue in my favor. "From what I have just seen—" he begins.

"Allow me to make things perfectly clear," my father interrupts. "Artemisia is entirely capable of carrying out the painting, but she will need my supervision."

"Very well, I'm in agreement with that. And afterward, I'll . . ."

"Afterward, if the painting is finished one day, it will naturally bear the signature of Gentileschi. I refuse to allow you to use my daughter as a . . . a freak attraction to help you get rich on our backs."

"If Artemisia paints a canvas, then it should be she who . . ."

"My daughter is part of my studio. For the time being she is simply one of my many apprentices. Even though she is perhaps the most talented one. But she is not even registered with the guild of Saint Luke yet. And it is I who am the master! If Artemisia accepts this order, my signature and mine alone will appear at the bottom of the piece!"

"You are allowing your pride to get the better of your judgment, Orazio. Consider what you have to gain instead. You have already proven yourself—no one questions your immense talent. Nevertheless, the Gentileschi studio is suffering from ever-growing competition. I must confess that it is becoming increasingly difficult to find clients who will accept you. They are all excited by young talent, everyone is drawn to new ideas, there's nothing I can do about it. Your daughter could—if you'll excuse the expression—revitalize the name of Gentileschi. Think of how beneficial it would be for the studio. And after all, it's only the first name that will change, the work shall still be stamped with the Gentileschi family seal!"

"I will not change my mind," my father retorts. "Either accept the order in my name, under the usual terms, or explain to the duke that I am too busy, and ask him to find another artist."

Complain as I may about his unfairness, and no matter how heatedly Nicolo bemoans the pity of it all, Orazio remains inflexible. I hardly recognize him. Papa has always protected and encouraged me. I tell myself that he must have his reasons, even if I can't imagine what they are. Could he be jealous of me? I can't bring myself to believe that. Nevertheless, I could swear that a hurt and defiant shadow sweeps over his face when, after Nicolo accepts his conditions, he growls, "So be it! . . . As for the profits from the painting, I will decide in due time what Artemisia's share will be."

The conversation ends there and Nicolo withdraws. He nonetheless manages to run into me the next day when I am alone. While I am still feeling saddened by this first disappointment in my father, Nicolo returns to the charge and evokes, in the most flattering of terms, the brilliant future and renown that, according to him, I have every right to aspire to.

"Don't worry," he murmurs. "I'll respect your father's wishes. But one can't keep certain rumors from getting about, can one? As the saying goes, truth always wins in the end."

I don't much like his cunning wink, filled with unspoken insinuations. It makes me feel guilty, full of ingratitude, as if I'm betraying Papa. And yet I silently acquiesce to Nicolo's suggestion.

Can he see what is in my heart? The man is quite sly. He immediately changes the subject and leads the conversation on to much more reassuring ground, evoking problems of a technical nature that might arise during the work.

Whom shall I take as a model for my Lucretia? He politely offers to send over some young women from whom I might choose. "That won't be necessary," I say. "I've already thought it over, I intend to pose for myself."

I explain the system of mirrors I have devised that will allow me to embody Lucretia. He seems delighted with the idea. "Now that will add a good deal of piquancy to the story when it comes to light, and contribute to your legend to boot. For not only will the world be able to admire your talent, but your great beauty as well."

Again the horrid wink that makes me feel as though I am stabbing my father in the back. Despite his flattering games, I'm no fool; Nicolo's sole motivation is self-gain. The day he discovers something even more extraordinary, a child of five painting with his toes, for example, he'll turn his back on me just as readily as he is doing with my father now.

As I walk him over to the garden fence, he draws a large florin from his purse and hands it to me. "A symbol," he says.

I gaze at the shiny gold piece. I should be dancing with delight, for I have never in my life had money in my possession. And yet I'm not in the least pleased. I say to myself, "I'm holding the deniers of Judas in my hand." And I run to the village church to slip the florin into the alms box.

I mustn't allow myself to be disheartened. I have to convince myself that it was my father who acted wrongly, that he is behaving like a tyrant, that he should have been proud that I was finally asked to sign a painting. I have to chase these dark thoughts from my mind, think only of my Lucretia.

With rapid strides I return to my studio and tie down the four flaps using the seaman's knots that Fulvio taught me.

First of all, I must allow myself to be completely inhabited by the character. Lying down on the couch in my studio, I go through the whole story once again, just as it took place in ancient Rome. It is essential to become immersed in one's subject. . . .

My name is Lucretia. This evening, my husband has been invited to a banquet. I am spinning wool as I await his return, keeping my eyes chastely upon my work, whereas my sisters-in-law are taking advantage of their husbands' absence and carousing with their lovers upstairs. I see the shadow of something moving under the closed door to my room.

They've already come to ask me to share in their revelry several times. This time, as before, I'll refuse. The door is thrown suddenly open. Terrified, I recognize the young Tarquinius, one of my husband's companions, followed by his Nubian slave. Why this brutal intrusion? What is the meaning of that peculiar look on his face? Has he come to make some terrible announcement? Has something happened to my husband? No, Tarquinius smashes one hand against my mouth, he raises his sword over my head. Has someone ordered my execution? One never knows, with all of the bloody intrigues that have become so commonplace in Rome of late. I kick and struggle, I don't want to die! At a brief order from his master, the African slave throws me upon the bed, holding my frantic, flailing limbs down with all of his savage strength.

Tarquinius stinks of wine, his voice is thick. "Your husband will pay for the wager he made! He swears upon your virtue. I have come to prove him wrong. I will have you one way or the other. Either you willfully consent to have me, or I will take you by force."

Taking his hand from my mouth he hisses, "Choose, Lucretia."

"Faced with adultery, I choose neither willful consent nor force. I would rather die!"

"You will not escape adultery, I have condemned you to that. If you refuse to surrender yourself to me, I will put you to the sword. You and my slave. I will lay your bodies side by side in such a position as to leave no doubt in anyone's mind. Then I will go out into Rome claiming that, having caught you fornicating, I took both your lives in vengeance for the adultery inflicted upon my dear friend, your loving husband, who will then pledge his everlasting gratitude to me. Decide what your fate will be, quickly!"

Horror-stricken, I allow him to do his will.

Several hours later, when my husband returns home, he finds me prostrate, trembling with fever, my tears run dry. I explain to him plainly the outrage that has been committed against me, and I await his punishment.

He does not chastise, but consoles me, "Only the mind can be the source of sin, Lucretia, not the body. You did not wish for this embrace, Tarquinius raped you. You are guilty of nothing. On the contrary, it is I who am to blame for it all. I made the stupid wager that if my comrades were to leave the banquet and go look in on their wives by surprise, they would find them in the very act of adultery. Tarquinius found his woman in the arms of another. Humiliated both by having been betrayed and losing his bet, furious at your reputed virtue, he took revenge upon you. Now he must pay for his crime.

My husband is a just man, full of benevolence. He has not deserved to have his honor sullied in this way. Even though I did not consent to the offense, I have lost the purity that he is entitled to expect of his wife. How can I live with my remorse? Without hesitating, I seize a dagger and plunge it into my heart. . . .

Thus perished the noble Lucretia . . . I sit suddenly up with a gasp, anxiously bring my hands to my breast. It's all right, I'm still alive. It takes me some time, however, before I recover completely from the nightmare, become Artemisia once again. Would I have reacted in the same way had Cosimo Quorli dishonored me? I don't believe so. I would have tried to live with my pain and, on the night of my wedding, I would have invented some huge lie. Each era has a different code of morality. I think about how I should depict the act of the Roman heroine. In those times, Christianity had not yet spread its beneficent wing over Italy. Suicide was not considered to be a mortal sin, depriving the victim of the right to burial and forbidding his entry into paradise, as it is today. On the contrary, it was seen as a courageous and noble act. In painting Lucretia's death, I would like to depict my own suicide, the one I will never commit. One of the marvelous things about painting is that it enables one to live certain experiences by proxy.

I imagine Lucretia alone, her clothing torn from her shoulders, exposing her breasts. She is sitting on the edge of the bed whose rumpled sheets suggest the outrage she has just undergone. The long tunic is pulled up, revealing a bare leg. The taught muscles in her thigh reflect her determination. The short sword is raised toward the heavens. She still hesitates. Her head is thrown backward, she has a worried expression on her face, as if she were questioning the gods. Already, her claw-like fingers are pulling at her left breast as if to punish her flesh and make room for the blade which will free her from this torture.

I run to get Fulvio to help adjust the mirror that will allow me to pose as Lucretia. I sum up the subject for him in a few words.

"So, I am going to see your breasts," he says happily.

I make a face at him. "Goodness, how exciting!"

"Well, I'm pleased about it all the same."

Placed at an angle in relation to the easel, the system of mirrors I've perfected gives me a three-quarters view, as if I were seeing myself from someone else's eyes. From this unaccustomed angle, with my torso emerging from a whirl of drapery, armed with the glaive, my throat exposed, I hardly recognize myself.

Several studies are scattered about. I can't decide which one of them to use. The arm held up straight seems too emphatic, yet with too much flexion, the gesture loses its poignancy. Taking up the pose again, I am attempting to find a middle ground when, reflected in one of the mirrors, I catch sight of a man's silhouette that I quickly recognize as Tassi.

If I can see him, it means that he sees me as well, with my bare breasts. As a matter of fact, his eyes have grown wide with surprise. I should be completely flustered at him seeing me like this, but I am so involved with my work that I don't allow my emotions to get the better of me this time.

Then a naughty idea crosses my mind. I murmur to Fulvio to come closer and, throwing my arms around his neck, I furtively slip my tongue into his mouth. How will my handsome adventurer react to this? I could have sworn that he suddenly grew pale, before turning and walking swiftly away.

He has barely disappeared when I push Fulvio away.

Still dazed by what I'd done and somewhat disoriented, my friend asks, "Whom was I being kissed by there? Was it Lucretia, Artemisia, or some other person you're pretending to be?"

"Let's start over again, all right? I would like you to move the central mirror slightly to the left." To myself, I say, *"I'm sorry, Fulvio. I just wanted to pay Tassi back. He made me jealous too the other day with Marisa. Now I know that I have the same power over him."*

24

Every minute of my time is devoted to Lucretia's suicide. The grand duke stipulated that the painting must be completed as quickly as possible; three months of work should suffice. Our client's haste amuses me: is the grand duchess so unfaithful that her husband wishes to hurriedly offer her this painting of Lucretia as an example of conjugal virtue?

Most people believe that a work of art is painted in less than no time, that the artist spends a moment in meditation and then suddenly allows his inspiration to run wild, that with a flick of the wrist, the painting is finished. They don't realize that painters work in two separate stages. First, the conception of the work of art, which is essentially a mental exercise as the great Leonardo used to say, and then the actual painting, which entails alternating periods of work with long hours of drying. The dark tones are always laid down first and, once it is certain that this base has hardened well, that it will not crack, the light areas are built up from it.

Should I retire from the world? Stop attending my lessons all together until I have finished with Lucretia? No. I'll see Tassi during the weeks of drying, that way, I won't waste any time. I'll ask my father to write a note of excuse for me and have Marisa deliver it. I prefer not to see Agostino in flesh and blood just now; I am afraid I might falter and slacken my pace.

Orazio comes barging into my studio every so often to check on my progress. He reminds me of a farmer picking up a laying hen to make sure the nest is full.

Though I feared I would miss Tassi to the point of not being able to think of anything else, I'm astonished to find it's not at all the case. To tell the truth, I hardly ever even think of him, my emotions seem to be hanging in suspense. Only at night does he come to join me in my dreams. In the morning, I've forgotten everything, but I awaken filled with his manly vigor and with the passion that he inspires in me. Does he actually love me? I'm not at all certain. I think that it is more likely that he finds me sexually arousing. Yes, it is desire rather than love. When I examine my own feelings, I find that I am caught up in a sort of gossamer webbing, a tangled multitude of threads, one more resistant than the other. I am growing dependent on him, that is for certain, but I can't analyze or describe the exact nature of this dependency. To me, Tassi represents the perfect mirror. In my father's eyes, I can see the reflection of a beloved child, a promising young artist, whereas the image of myself that I perceive in Agostino's face is more complete, a woman and a painter at the same time, body and soul. And the woman in me would like very much to encounter the man in Tassi.

I am sweating profusely in Lucretia's paint-stained robe, my hair sticking to my temples, I rise from my work every now and again to adjust the height of the chandelier or the position of a mirror that a breath of wind has displaced, I must look like a very rough sketch of the Roman heroine.

Days follow one after the other. The face is taking on form. I have finished the first layer of the drapery, colored in the rounded shape of the thigh, applied the large flat surface of the background. The paint is beginning to stick to the brush; it is impossible to continue to work with the fresh paint any longer. Finally, I lay down my paintbrushes.

In a little while, Vito will help me take the canvas up to my room, where it will be able to dry free of dust.

25

"The master is at the work site," Batisto informs me. "He asked for you to wait for him. He won't be long."

While Marisa and the main assistant go sit on the edge of the well—apparently to flirt with each other, since my chaperone is all aflutter with girlish giggles—I open my portfolio. The young apprentice who is napping on the terrace, naked to the waist, with his face half hidden under his arm, is an excellent subject for a sketch, a good way to keep myself busy while awaiting my professor's return.

"How do you manage to capture physical emotion so well, without knowing the vast possibilities that the body offers?"

I keep myself from starting in surprise. Tassi is standing there behind me, and I didn't hear him walk up. "I never said that I didn't know."

If the tone of my voice is affected, it is in order to hide the overwhelming feeling of shyness that has suddenly come over me. Agostino seems to be deeply disturbed, or am I imagining things? He has the same expression of all-consuming jealousy on his face that he did the day I kissed Fulvio just for his sake. In a gnashing, strangled voice he fumes, "I certainly would like to know who posed for those studies in the nude that you showed me."

A thought flashes through my mind: a lover's quarrel. And I want to reassure him, repair the senseless wrong that I have done him. Unlike Lucretia, I tell myself, my body hasn't sinned, but I committed adultery in my soul. And I was equally unfaithful to Agostino in my mind, with Fulvio on paper, using a lead crayon. How muddled it all is in my head! At times like this it's as if someone else, a secret Artemisia, hidden deep within me, is speaking and acting in my place.

Abruptly, I hear myself murmur, "Would you like to pose for me?" And I add, dropping my eyes, "I don't mean in the nude."

The question popped our unexpectedly without my even thinking about it. I anxiously search his face that suddenly resembles a battle-field upon which a thousand conflicting ideas are clashing. The tempest gradually dies down, now he is looking at me very gravely, but with a slight smile at the corners of his mouth.

He calls to Marisa, "Go and find something to clean up, my girl!"

The unfortunate chaperone casts a perplexed gaze about the immaculately kept terrace, shrugs her shoulders in frustration. Agostino hands her a broom and nudges her gently toward the beach. "Why yes, of course, just look out there—there's all of that sand that needs sweeping."

Stupefied, Marisa plods away, dragging the broom behind her, as Tassi and I walk into the studio. The shutters are closed and the large room is bathed in a thick half-light. Nevertheless, as soon as I notice the bed with the bust of the sea nymph, I have a very clear vision: Agostino will pose as Holofernes, and I will be Judith. Judith decapitating Holofernes. I have been haunted by the subject ever since I admired that painting by Caravaggio, at the Academy in Rome. Yes, it is the very same bed as in my dream, and Holofernes has Tassi's features in the dream, and I am Judith. How could I have repressed that vision, pushed it into the forgotten recesses of my mind? Although I don't understand the reason for it, I carry this painting within me as one does a child. What mysterious bonds tie me to the Jewish heroine? Why should Agostino deserve the same punishment as Holofernes? I try to recall the essentials of Judith's story. It takes place long before the birth of Christ, in the town of Bethulia, in Judaea. The army of Holofernes, Nebuchadnezzar's general, is besieging the town. A widow by the name of Judith receives an order from God to save her people. She leaves the city accompanied by her servant and goes to the camp of the Assyrians. Brought before Holofernes, she captivates him with her beauty and induces him to drink. The general soon falls prey to the vapors of alcohol. Inebriated, he sprawls out on his bed. Then, instead of joining him, the beautiful Jewess cuts off his head and carries it away with her. The next morning the Jews of Bethulia hang the bloody trophy from the gates to the city. The demoralized Assyrians, dissipate, and beat a retreat.

The whole story passes through my mind as I lead Agostino over to the bed with the bust of the sea nymph. He doesn't yet know what I have in mind, and docilely allows me to guide him. I ask him to unfasten his shirt and lie down on the bed.

"Let your head hang back over the edge. Lift your arms as if you were struggling against an enemy."

Without taking his eyes from mine, Tassi takes the pose. The look in his eyes is gentle, so infinitely gentle, it moves me, yet it is not what I want. "Not like that," I say curtly. "I want something more intense."

And, feigning to strike him with an invisible sword, I insist, "Act as if you were really trying to defend yourself from me! You are Holofernes, Judith has beguiled you, she is not bringing the kisses you had hoped for, but death . . ."

Instinctively, he grabs my wrists. Not in order to push me away, but to pull me toward him. Still, he doesn't allow my body to tumble down upon his, he catches my fall. I am hit by a blinding thunderbolt, the feeling is completely new, a volcanic eruption leaving a trickle of lava running into my abdomen. Agostino sits up quickly, as if he has guessed what I'm feeling, and is afraid of his own acts. The expression on his face changes all of a sudden, and in an icy voice he says, "It is time to go now. The lesson is finished."

I feel as though I've committed a crime of some sort. Embarrassed and ashamed, I hastily gather my things up and leave the room.

26

This morning, when we met again, it was as if nothing had happened between us two days ago. Agostino was in a gay mood, relaxed, the expression on his face was almost childlike. He had even made a little kite out of blue paper to show me how to play with the wind. Costanza, his ex-mistress, was idling around aimlessly a short distance away. At one point, she approached us and I was struck as much by her beauty as by the sadness in her face that she tries to conceal by affecting an air of detachment.

"Are you feverish?" she asked Agostino in a heavily ironic voice, and placed her hand on his moist brow.

My adventurer pulled away shaking his head. "I've never seen you like this," she went on, still mockingly. "So, now you've taken to making toys?"

Seeing our embarrassment, she burst out laughing and resumed her teasing. "To see all the trouble you go to, one can't help but think you are actually jealous of the young fisherman who pines after Artemisia. Don't get your hopes up too high, you're no longer sixteen years old, dear!"

Upon pronouncing this last spiteful remark, and seeing from my expression that I fully understood that Tassi confided in her, Costanza turned and walked off toward the village.

Agostino continued flying his kite, but absentmindedly, without the slightest enthusiasm. With a closed face and a wild look in his eyes, he suddenly turned to Marisa, placed in her hands the ball of string at the end of which his paper bird was soaring, and took me by the wrist.

He is pulling me along by the hand. He's walking very rapidly, I have to run to keep up. I turn around to see Marisa playing with the kite, and I would like to cling to that vision of carefree innocence, as though I've had the presentiment that something is going to break. Already we are crossing the flagstone floor of the terrace. We enter the studio.

I still don't understand what Tassi wants of me. I suppose he wishes to talk to me alone, to reiterate what he told me the first time, that dealing with one Gentileschi is already complicated enough, that our relationship as master and student is taking an unacceptable turn, that women are definitely a plague for him. I tell myself that he is going to send me away, order me to go back to my apprenticeship with my father, implore me to never come back and bother him again—I'm sure of it. Why has he turned the key in the lock? Why is he holding me so tightly to his breast? I don't quite understand, I'm not ready yet, I'm frightened, my pulse is beating wildly, I'm fighting him.

Without listening to my protests, he is nibbling at the back of my neck, calling me his little wildcat, unlacing my corset, kissing my shoulders, coming back up to my neck. He seeks out my mouth, finds it, spreads my lips, makes his way between my teeth. I am suffocating. His tongue winds around mine, two muscles wrestling. Gradually, I am weakening, torn between the panic that this all too sudden unleashing of passion inspires in me, and the drunkenness of desire mounting in my own body, fearing that perhaps I cannot satisfy his ardor, dreading that he will then turn away from me—the innocent young thing, incapable of being a real woman—that he will disappear from my life forever.

I never would have believed he would declare his passion for me in this manner. I expected sweet words, words that would make me melt. Silently, he pushes me hurriedly up against the wall, pulls up my skirts, and spreads my legs. I want to flee.

Then why am I unable to push him away? Is it possible to desire and refuse something at the same time?

My body falls limp in his arms, tears fill my eyes. I must have lost consciousness for a few instants. He has lifted me up, my feet are no longer touching the floor. Now he is gently laying me down on the bed with the sea nymph's bust. I feel as though I'm his child, or plunder he has taken in a battle. My right thigh is jerking with a nervous tick. He gently brushes away the strand of hair covering part of my face and places a kiss on my forehead.

"There now, calm down."

I close my eyes and wait. His voice fades away under my skirts, becomes muffled in the intimate folds of flesh between my legs. All I am able to do is to repeat, "No, no . . ." Is he even listening to me? The coarseness of his beard makes the inside of his mouth seem all the more silken and soft. His hands are everywhere. I would like to cry out to him to stop. Instead, I am moaning with pleasure, my eyes close, my neck twists, my back arches and my whole body convulses like a carp being pulled out of the water on the end of a line. My hips thrust forward involuntarily, and my fists pummel his shoulders.

Against my will, I am floating in absolute bliss. It is a whole new world in which there is no place for modesty. I am almost disappointed when the feeling slowly ebbs. Why is he moving back up toward my face, lifting himself away from me?

And then I scream! The cry is a mixture of surprise and pain. I scratch at Agostino's face. I jump up from the bed. I see the red stain on the white sheet. I slip my fingers between my legs, and when I look at them, they are covered with blood.

"You've hurt me!"

"I'm sorry . . . I had no idea. I thought that . . ."

My hands lash out at his face, striking it with every ounce of my strength, over and over, giving free rein to all of my pent-up fear and rage. He doesn't try to defend himself, doesn't say a word. With tears clouding his eyes, he watches me returning hurt for hurt. My blows grow weaker and weaker. The last slap is practically a caress. I crumple on the bed in tears. What has he done to me?

Agostino takes my bloody hand and lays it on his cheek. "I love you, Artemisia." The blood from my lost virginity streaks his face, runs into the scratch marks I left there. I love him too. And I hate him just as much. Why must our love be a pact sealed in blood?

With water from the pitcher, my lover gently washed my loins. When it was time for us to part, he told me that I had haunted his thoughts more than anyone ever had before. I could have paid him exactly the same compliment.

With my legs still wobbly, I go outside to join Marisa. I see the look in her eyes. Marisa is the outside world, the world that views lovemaking before marriage as the most unforgivable of sins. I nearly burst out in tears. She doesn't make a single remark, simply straightens out my clothing with the protective gestures of a big sister. Does she know? Regardless of what she has understood, even if she disapproves of me, I get the feeling that she does not judge me, but accepts what has happened, that she's on my side. I know that Marisa will keep quiet. Anyone else wouldn't have been motivated by the feeling of reciprocal loyalty that exists between young women of the same age. God, please let me not be pregnant! God, please never let anyone know what I have just done.

"It's time to go," she says, adjusting her own mantilla on my shivering shoulders.

We walk along in silence. Marisa is the first to open the door to our house and, upon Tuzia's order, hurries off to peel the vegetables for the midday meal. Alone in the little entryway, I lean on the banister to the staircase, my forehead resting on the large copper ball. What will ever become of me? If Agostino doesn't marry me, I am a lost woman, ruined. To most people, I am already handicapped by the fact that I'm a painter, but who would want a . . .

My father's voice interrupts my somber thoughts. "Misia, come here, I need your help!"

I turn around with a jump, panicking. The crime must surely be written all over my face, the smell of my lover must be emanating from the folds in my clothing. But no, Orazio doesn't notice any of these things.

"You aren't going to go and fall asleep on your feet now, are you? Come and give me a hand in the studio, you can take a nap later on."

Make-believe for everyone, appear to be the same as before, smile, affect temper tantrums, play the naive child.

Then night came. Finally alone, hugging the cushion, sleep brought me the memory of Agostino's skin. He and I were the couple lying there on the beach. I was the girl who was moaning in the sand. Lying over my body, Agostino was murmuring, "I'll never leave you, I want to marry you, to live with you." In the morning, I awoke with the feather cushion between my legs jammed up against my genitals, and my pelvis making little back and forth movements.

27

For several days I was smitten with remorse, then I returned. Now I am the one who initiates the caresses, who asks for more, who invents new approaches.

Lying naked on my lover's wide bed, still numb with pleasure, I am watching him contemplate me. I adore the dark circles that form around his eyes after making love. He prowls around me like a wild animal, he roars and shows his teeth. He pretends to pounce on me and begin devouring my breast, as if he were quarreling over a piece of meat with another lion.

"My dearest little moon, you drive me to such distraction that I almost forget that I'm your professor. Say we'll begin our lessons again, will you? Today I'll teach you the thirty-three canons of feminine beauty, as defined by Morgupo in his *Costume de la donne.*"

And, suiting the action to the word, interrupting himself to kiss, sniff, lick each and every one of my attributes, Agostino proclaims:

"What are the measurements of the ideal body?

Three long ones: the hair, the hands, and the legs.

Three tiny ones: the teeth, the ears, and the breasts.

Three broad ones: the forehead, the torso, and the hips.

Three elongated, but well-proportioned ones: the height, the arms, and the thighs.

Three fine ones: the eyebrows, the fingers, and the lips.

Three small ones: the mouth, the chin and the feet.

Three white ones: the teeth, the throat, and the hands.

Three red ones: the cheeks, the lips, and the nipples.

Three narrow ones: the waist, the knees, and 'the place in which nature has put everything soft.'

Three black ones: the brows, the eyes, and 'you know what.'

Three round ones: the neck, the arms, and the . . ."

I stretch lazily. "Professor, how would you grade your student?"

"Morgupo would give you thirty out of thirty-three, because your hips are as narrow as a young boy's, your breasts are too ample, your lips too full. But I award you first prize!" And we make love once again.

28

I meet with Agostino early every morning and leave him only come nightfall. To keep my father from suspecting anything, I explained to him that as long as I could not begin a second coat of paint on my Lucretia, and since the same thing was true of the frescoes that Tassi is painting on the ceiling of the church, my teacher had kindly offered to give me full-time lessons in the meanwhile. Orazio was overjoyed at the honor paid to his daughter. If he knew the extent of the dishonor . . .

My lover is initiating me to the secrets of my own body and of his, teaching me to keep our movements in time with each other. He leads me to discover something that I never imagined possible: amity between a man and a woman, the communion of souls over and above that of the flesh. We are also accomplishing quite a bit of work. Interspersing our amorous bouts with long sittings. The painting of Judith and Holofernes is therefore coming along quite rapidly, even though at times I can't resist straddling the man that I'm supposedly beheading, sitting down on his male member and writhing lasciviously until it becomes hard and erect and penetrates me.

This new work is very important to me. Much more so than Lucretia is, even though I know that as soon as the first layer of paint has been applied, I will have to give up coming to the white house, go back to my studio, and devote myself exclusively to finishing Nicolo's order.

So as not to think about it, or to ward off the fated day, I concentrate on depicting the extreme violence of this scene in all of its horror, on portraying the physical difficulty that Judith encounters in cutting through Holofernes's thick neck, on trying to infer the sound of the blade separating the vertebrae, on conveying the mixture of disgust and excitement that this barbarous act inspires in the biblical heroine. The blood gushes out—so much blood. Holofernes' eyes are blaze with surprised horror. Perhaps it is my way of taking revenge on Agostino, who has taken possession of me, body and soul. A way of declaring my autonomy. As dependent as I am on him, I am still strong enough to free myself of him whenever I wish. In truth, I pray that our destinies will be inseparable, that he will take me for his wife, and who knows? Perhaps I shall give him a son, but I don't dare bring up the subject. We live in a secret little world of our own, far from the prying eyes of others, and I'm afraid that if I tell him what is troubling me, I will break the magic spell. Agostino controls my future; I just can't help resenting the power he has over me. What will become of me if he doesn't marry me? The prospect fills me with horror. Thankfully, I have Marisa's support. Our relationship changed after that first time with Tassi, or more exactly, that's when it was born. She's become a friend to me, an ally. To think that I used to believe she was dimwitted! How blind I was, how narrow-minded! I have since learned to know her; to appreciate her sensitivity, her common sense. As a matter of fact, it is she who taught me how to minimize my risk of getting pregnant. She is also the one who acts as a lookout for my lover and me, shielding us from potential dangers. What goes through Marisa's mind during the long hours she spends tramping about in the sand on the beach? Is she herself living my love affair by proxy and intensely enjoying it? Or are our lives so very different that, free as a bird, she entrusts her personal dreams to the little blue paper kite that Tassi gave her, flying so very high up in the sky? I hope, for her sake, the latter is the case.

29

My womb has not swollen, no one suspects my liaison with Agostino, and our lovemaking grows more passionate as time goes on. Our being separated enhanced it as well: the several weeks we were apart, during which I went back to my studio to work on *Lucretia,* only accentuated the magnetic attraction we feel for each other. There has still been no mention of marriage though. It is, so to speak, the only dark cloud in the picture. *Judith and Holofernes* is nearly finished. As for the *Lucretia,* Nicolo, my father's agent, will soon be able to come and pick it up. The grand duke will offer it to his wife on the appointed date. I venture to trust that her highness will be completely satisfied with it.

When I showed him the progress I was making in my work, Papa thoroughly complimented me and once again mentioned our never-ending partnership. I only pray that our filial felicity is not destroyed by Nicolo's schemes. I haven't forgotten the Machiavellian look on his face the day that he said certain rumors could not be helped. Though in my despicable vanity, regardless of the love I feel for Papa, I would like for the truth to come out. I am appalled at the thought of betraying him in this way.

More troublesome is the fear that Orazio will learn how I spend the better part of my days. Even though I am confident that Marisa will keep the secret, it seems to me that Batisto, on the other hand, my lover and master's assistant, is entirely capable of spilling the beans if he could in any way gain from it. I haven't been able to get it off of my mind for the last few days, ever since Papa greeted me in such a strange manner one day as I came back from the white house. He never interferes with what Tassi teaches me, for I believe that he is both happy and a bit annoyed that someone else is responsible for instilling the secrets of art in me, yet he was standing in the little vestibule, awaiting my return, with his arms crossed and a dark look on his face.

"So, what did our friend from Florence teach you today?" he asked pointedly.

Affecting the most self-assured attitude in the world, I answered without hesitating, "Perspective, Papa." And sketching a quick diagram in the air with my finger, I added, "The lines all converge at the horizon. Like this!"

Orazio didn't pay the least attention to my explanation. He was scrutinizing Marisa carefully, his brows lifted as if in inquiry. The poor chaperone was squirming uncomfortably. Would she succumb and cause the downfall of us all?

"It seems that you've been out in the sun," my father remarked in a suspicious tone of voice.

Marisa stammered something unintelligible. I realized I had to come to the rescue quickly. "The horizon can only be studied out-of-doors, Father. We were painting landscapes, that is why . . ."

"Yet your skin hasn't tanned at all."

"It's because I was sitting under the parasol we use to protect the canvas and the pigments."

I was able to cut the unpleasant scene short that time, but still, on several occasions since then, Orazio has given me some very perplexed looks that continue to worry me. I vow to be extra careful from now on. Does he suspect something? Has someone talked? How can I find out? No, it just isn't possible . . . I'm imagining things, he certainly doesn't know anything at all."

30

What could be more beautiful, more mysterious, more inspiring than an herbarium? The fragments of nature presented therein are so familiar and yet, taking them out of context, mounting them on a neutral background, renders them deeply enigmatic, reveals just what an artist God is. How infinite the imagination to have conceived such a variety of forms!

While Agostino reads off the strange names of the dried plants and flowers that he collects in a large, leather-bound album, I am wishing I could share these feelings of awestruck admiration with Marisa. Some of the plants come from across the Alps, still others from beyond the seas.

Naked, sitting with our legs crossed on the large, mussed bed, one by one, we lift the sheets of waxed paper upon which he has mounted his astonishing harvest toward the light dappling in from the closed shutters. Agostino shares in my delight, or rather he seems delighted that I am so fascinated.

Marisa just has to see this. I run to open the window and call to her, but the beach is deserted, so is the terrace. I could have sworn I heard her just a little while ago. Where could she have gone?

Hastily dressed again, without bothering to explain to Agostino why I am in such a sudden hurry, I look everywhere for her. Marisa has disappeared. An awful feeling of dread comes over me. In the back of my mind I know that something terrible must have happened. My lover doesn't understand my panic. He tries to hold me back with kisses. "Your chaperone was undoubtedly tired of waiting for you," he says lightly. "She'll come back soon."

I finish fixing my tousled hair. Unable to appease me, Agostino accuses me of "deserting him." "I'll see you tomorrow!" he says, giving me one last kiss.

"Tomorrow? I don't know. I . . . my father . . ."

"Your father will find it strange if you don't come."

Without losing another second, I rush back toward the house as quickly as my legs will carry me. Having run all the way, I am frozen dead in my tracks a few feet from home. Raised voices are coming from the garden.

Feeling as though I am suffocating, panting heavily, my entire body is soaked in sweat, I can hear Papa's voice. "What have you done, you miserable wretch? What in God's name have you done? Answer me!"

Marisa does not respond. She is sobbing, frozen with fear and incapable of knowing what to say.

"I confided my daughter to your care, and you have given her away. You are Tassi's procuress!"

"No, it's not true, I swear it!" my chaperone finally mumbles.

"I should take the whip to you. How could you have done this? How much did he offer you to deliver her up to him? And I, who trusted you . . . Harlot, she-devil!"

He beats Marisa, who only weeps pitifully and repeats that she has done nothing wrong, until Papa finally stomps out of the house, his face distorted with rage.

I see him rush past only a few cubits from the woodpile, behind which I just had time enough to hide. What had happened? Who had betrayed us? I can still hear Marisa whimpering, but I simply cannot move. I stand there for a long time breathing in the smell of freshly cut wood, the odor of sap that is so invigorating and from which I hope to draw a bit of courage. I must get my thoughts back in order. Since my father is gone, I don't have to face him right away. I know him. I know that as usual, just as he does every time he loses his temper, or something terrible has happened, or he needs to make an important decision, he will go off to wander around in the pine woods, or even out as far as the marshland, and won't come back until nightfall, calmer but also more determined. This respite will allow me to get my thoughts together and organize my defense.

I leave my hiding place. Curled up on her pallet under the stairs, Marisa is trembling like a leaf. She doesn't seem surprised to see that I have already come back from Tassi's house. I lie down next to her, dry her tears, and hug her very tightly. Her nose is running, with the skirt of my dress, I wipe it clean.

"I was playing with the kite," she starts to explain in great heaving sobs. "I didn't hear your father arrive. And when I saw him, it was too late to stop him or to warn you. He peered through the stained glass of the window, motioning me to keep quiet. I'm not the one who alerted him, I swear. He had come out by chance, he wanted to ask something of Tassi. It's not my fault."

"I know, Marisa, I know."

"He said that I would go to prison for having helped Agostino to seduce you."

"No one will go to prison."

"He said that I'm no good. That they will brand me with a hot iron."

"Now, now, don't be silly . . ."

I rock my friend in my arms to console her, and finally, exhausted with emotion, she drifts off to sleep. That is when I truly become petrified. Dear God, it was such a beautiful day, my adventurer and I had worked side by side, made love, contemplated the beauties and the mysteries of creation in his herbarium—there's nothing reprehensible about any of that—and then . . . I suddenly realize how truly terrible the consequences of my crime are.

Young Vito is hopping about like an imp. He had no trouble in flushing us out from the recess under the stairs where we had dug in. It's obvious he knows something. "Come on!" he exclaims, pulling us both along by one hand.

"What is it? Tell us, now!"

"Not here, Tuzia might hear us."

We slip out of the house and go to the back of the garden to hold our conference, far from any eavesdroppers. Night has already fallen. Outside in the moonlight, Vito prances around even more impatiently. "I can't stay long, I'm on watch at the work site. I was able to slip away in secret, but I will have to go back soon."

One would almost think that the turn of events amuses him. Due to his young age, he probably has no idea of the gravity of the situation. As always, so as not to omit a single remark and tell us everything that he heard in scrupulous detail, he imitates the people whose conversation he wishes to relate. But today I'm in no mood to admire his talent. Damn his play-acting!

"I was over in the corner washing the paintbrushes," he says. "Master Tassi was up at the very top of the scaffolding and was painting the vault in the candlelight, lying down on a board. Your father barges furiously in, bellowing, 'Agostino! Agostino!' And when Tassi tells him he is working, your father roars even louder, 'You worm, get down here immediately!' Tassi simply puts down his brushes, and remains perched in his place. 'How dare you have touched my daughter? You have nothing to say in answer? You who pretended to be my friend? If you have abused her then you must keep her and take her as your wife. It is the only way out, the only means by which to spare us shame and dishonor, and to keep yourself out of prison. Do you hear me, filthy animal? You will marry her!'"

As he tells his story, Vito puffs out his sunken cheeks exaggeratedly, and he mimes my father's both furious and pained look so well, imitates his stuttering and each of his intonations with such genuine talent, that I feel as though I am actually watching the scene.

"What did Tassi say?" I ask, cutting him off impatiently.

"Nothing."

"What do you mean, nothing?"

"Nothing, that's all. He was half hidden in the shadows. Your father began shaking the scaffolding like a madman. The candles, the palette, the pigments, all of your master's material came tumbling to the floor. I was afraid that the whole structure would come crashing down on Master Orazio's head."

"And Tassi didn't say anything?"

"Not a word. He must have been too frightened."

I don't understand my lover's attitude. It's not like him to be frightened; he fears nothing and no one. So why this silence when faced with my father's despair? One word would have been enough to appease him. Why hadn't my adventurer simply promised him to put the ring on my finger? Orazio would have raged around a little longer, just out of principle, and then they would have toasted to our happiness. He has a lot of respect for Agostino, he told me so once. I am convinced that he would be proud to have him as his son-in-law. And even more so since the marriage would improve the Gentileschi studio by adding a choice recruit: Agostino Tassi, nothing to sniff at.

Vito is speaking in his normal voice now. All of a sudden he scowls. "Your father was weeping with rage, Misia. He kept repeating, 'You can't do this to me! You can't do this to me!' He turned back toward Tassi one last time and cried, 'Coward! God will never forgive you!' and I heard him hiss between his teeth, 'And neither will I.'"

And neither will I . . . These last words torment me. Thus Papa intends to take revenge upon my lover. My mind is buzzing fretfully and I am assailed with an abominable vision: it is no longer Judith who is decapitating Holofernes, but Orazio Gentileschi. A grotesque rictus deforms my father's face as the blade of his sword slices through Agostino's neck.

The vision pushes my hurried footsteps out to the white house on the beach. I want to save my adventurer, beg him, plead with him on bended knees to flee the house, to go as far away as possible. Perhaps I could join him later, in France or Spain. But I would prefer never seeing him again to knowing he were in danger. Our marriage, the child that I would have liked for him to give me, my hopes of our living together, all of that is insignificant in view of the urgent situation. Protecting him from my father's vengeance is the only thing of any importance now.

I run, struggling against the newly risen north wind blowing in gales as though it hoped to counter my wishes and hold back my steps. The gusts alternately make my dress either billow out or cling to my legs. The clouds hide the stars, and all of a sudden it is very dark. Several times, bumping into invisible obstacles—a stone, a root—I stumble, fall, skin my hands and knees. Now there is blood running down my calf, my heart is racing. I redouble my efforts. Never has the path, cherished up until this very morning and traveled with joy, seemed so long, so loathsome. The road to happiness has become for me like the passion of Christ. Is it even certain that I will find Agostino at home? Instinctively, I believe I will. Going by the work site would simply hold me up. I sense that danger is imminent; I am frightened for the man that I love. Finally, a dip in the crestline of the dune allows me to glimpse the sea; the white house is not far now.

Without stopping to catch my breath, I run on when, unexpectedly, I hear the whickering of a horse. Has Agostino somehow intimated my plan? Is he preparing to flee into exile? Several silhouettes are scuffling in front of the porch; at first I can only make out a confused commotion. There are some men and three, no, four horses. Is he taking his assistants with him in his flight? Again, I stumble on an uneven piece of ground, sprain my ankle, fall headlong into a bush. Now I can distinguish the echo of voices that I don't recognize. The torchlight glints sharply from a steel helmet. They are wearing breastplates, carrying pikes, swords. In a flash, I realize I have come too late. Absolutely helpless, I witness Agostino's arrest.

Standing between two armed guards, with his hands tied behind his back, he looks like a condemned prisoner. An officer barks out an order and the small troop marches off. The wind stifles my screams.

Where are they taking him? What will they do to him? They have already gone quite some distance, leaving me alone in my suffering and despair. Agostino hasn't committed any sin, any crime. All he is guilty of is smothering me in love, in happiness, and in pleasure. What penalty does he face? Why did he seem to be walking to the gallows between those two guards? It is true that I am a minor, true that he took me by surprise if not by force while I was still a virgin, true that he transgressed the trust that my family had placed in him. But can he not redeem himself from his faults in the same way that he redeemed himself for his brutality with me, the second time, when he taught me what love is? He must know that everything will turn out all right in the end. In a few days, Papa will go and see him behind bars and will ask him to marry me again and, if only to regain his liberty, he will consent. Why hadn't that fool agreed in the first place? If he so abhors the idea of marriage, for reasons that escape me, we will exchange our rings before the priest and, afterward, protected by the sacred ties, I will grant him the freedom to do as he pleases. The idea that, faced with my father's virulence at the church, his silence had been inspired by a lack of love for me, or was due to the fact that he was tiring of me, or still yet that he preferred one of his past mistresses to me, had occurred to me, I admit, but without my really being able to believe it. My adventurer is not as talented an actor as Vito is. Only a few hours ago he had sworn his love for me in a tone that cannot be mistaken. Some sort of agreement will be reached and the matter will be taken care of on friendly terms, I'm sure. Maybe we will even be able to keep it all quiet, avoid a scandal. . . . What could possibly keep Agostino from marrying me? I wouldn't demand his continuous presence, or even money, for I have my painting. No, I want nothing, nothing but for him to be set free. If he so much as asks me, I will cast the chains that my father wishes to fetter him with, both literally and figuratively, far from us. I will be his Penelope and, while I am waiting, he can travel around the world and back again, if that's what suits him, just like Ulysses.

3 1

From the kitchen window, I can see my father and Tuzia in the midst of a heated discussion. My stepmother is in her nightgown and bonnet. As for Orazio, he hasn't changed yet. Sitting wild-eyed across from his wife, his fists clenched on the oaken table, his jaw drawn tight, not finding words harsh enough to describe Tassi's conduct, he launches into a string of lamentations about the misfortune that has befallen his household.

I'm not afraid of his wrath. I'm filled with bitter resentment and make as dignified an entrance as my soiled robe and dirty face will permit.

"What have you done, Papa?" I demand irately.

He glowers at me, and when he answers my question, his speech impediment seems more pronounced than ever. "I have acted as the head of this family, nothing more. I was duty-bound to chasten that brute, that traitor. To think that I once called him my friend, that I had entrusted your education to him . . ."

"But I'm in love with him! And he loves me as well!"

"Silly child!"

My father stands up and shakes me as if he wanted me to swallow the words I had spoken.

"What do you know of love? You're only a child. He raped you, that is the fact of the matter. Never would Orazio Gentileschi's daughter have allowed herself to be seduced before marriage! He raped you I tell you!"

I glare at him steadily—squarely in the eyes. "The only thing he did was to give me pleasure."

The slap comes so quickly, is so hard, that my cheek hardly feels the impact at all. It simply grows numb, and so I don't even feel the pain either. I just have the bizarre sensation of having a double row of teeth on the left side of my mouth. Defiantly, I turn my right cheek, "Go ahead, strike me again if it will make you feel better!"

Orazio lifts his hands to his hair, as if to rip it out, then sits back down and without looking at me again, says to Tuzia, "Talk to her. I can get nowhere."

My stepmother tries to take the gentle approach. "If you explain to them that he raped you . . ."

"Shut up! You have no place telling me what to do. Sleeping with my father does not make you my mother! And for that matter, to whom am I supposed to claim that he raped me?"

"To the law," my father answers in a defeated voice. "Only they can force him to marry you."

"To the law," I shudder. "So you intend to charge him?"

"Misia, it's for your own good, it's to save the honor of our family, your honor . . ."

"Isn't it rather to keep everything to yourself, your daughter and the frescoes for Monte Cavallo, which you never really accepted sharing with Agostino? Now it is you who are betraying him! You said you were his friend, but you were simply waiting for the first opportunity to avenge your wounded pride. It always rankled you that, by order of the Pope, the major part of the order was assigned to our friend from Florence, as you call him! Now what you would like above all, in my opinion, is to put him in prison, ruin his reputation, and finish the frescoes yourself!"

This time it is not just a slap that my outburst has earned me but a full front and back hand-lashing that sends me flying, knocking my head up against the sink.

Unable to sleep, I spent the whole night sobbing, biting my pillow, and calling out, "Mama, Mama," just like a frightened child, something I hadn't done since I left the convent. It also occurred to me how utterly pathetic I was, clinging to my cushion as though it were a plank at sea. I was filled with rancor toward my father for having destroyed my happiness, for having rent open the horror-filled chasm at my feet. And there was my rancor toward Agostino, too, for having allowed things to go this far, and toward myself for not being stronger, for having so little control over my own destiny. Finally, I was vehemently bitter about God's laws and those of man as well, about the world as a whole. Because of all of them, because of their accursed intolerance, my entire existence was to crumble like an old ruin, and my life had only just begun. Barely seventeen years old and already I am brokenhearted, have compromised my reputation, am completely disillusioned by the human race, have a family on the verge of repudiating me and, maybe, God only knows, a bastard in my belly.

When morning comes, my future seems as black as pitch, and as uncertain as a peace treaty with the Turks. But I know I won't surrender without a fight. Artemisia Gentileschi will recover her dignity! And if the world rejects me today, I will at least try to live, far from its iniquity, and leave a favorable impression for posterity. When I have exhausted the very last ounce of my strength trying to save Tassi, I will fight on for myself with the only arms I am familiar with—my paintbrushes dipped in the blood of pigment.

32

One Sunday, as we were leaving mass, two soldiers from the Papal Guard, dressed in their handsome yellow uniforms, designed by the famous Michelangelo, served us with a summons. Agostino Tassi's trial was to begin the next day. I was requested to appear in Orazio's company.

Tuzia spent the whole day letting out a very childish white dress trimmed with red ribbons that I haven't worn since the day I left for the convent. My father actually wants me to wear it! Does he really think I can't see through his little tricks? I'm not so stupid as to be blind to the stratagem. Lily-white purity and innocence, shot with red ribbons, the blood of my shame. On top of it all, he asks me to wear my hair in two braids hanging down on either side of my face, just as preadolescent girls do. I will have nothing to do with this imposture, and slip my everyday dress back on, put a little rouge on my lips and cheeks, some shadow on my eyes. Without wanting to appear to be a light woman, I will not cheat. The judge will see me just as Tassi sees me— as I am. I refuse to play the virtuous child; it would only aggravate Agostino's case.

The hired carriage came for us at dawn. It is taking us toward Rome, toward the Court of Justice. The single seat is so narrow that, in order to avoid physical contact with my father, I must squeeze myself up against the door. I don't utter a word during the whole journey. An obstinate frown creases my brow and my eyes take on a vacant gaze.

Orazio's obvious discomfort fills the cab with a heavy atmosphere. He looks as if he's aged ten years. He seems disoriented, unhappy, almost unsure of himself. I certainly hope he isn't expecting me to say something placating of all things, even if he is still my father, the person I cherished most in the whole world, whom I revered as highly as I did God himself. Hate has entered my heart and spread like a terrible poison. A few of the old, loving reflexes continue nevertheless to struggle against this venom. They flare up, brandishing the illusion in which I would still like to believe despite everything—assuring me that everything will be all right in the end, that things will take their normal course once again. No, in all honesty, I can't allow myself to be deluded by this fallacy any longer. Even if Agostino consents to marrying me, I know I'll never be able to forget Orazio's infamous conduct. I will never forgive him.

The heat inside the cab is suffocating; I'm drenched with sweat. Papa offers me a drink from his leather bottle. A slight shrug of the shoulders is my sole response for, despite my dry, burning throat, I have decided that I will never accept anything coming from him again.

We have left the countryside and are driving through the city already. I hadn't even noticed. There is a large crowd gathered outside of the Court of Justice. Why such a throng? It's not market day today. Maybe some high-ranking dignitary is visiting, a foreign prince passing through Rome? Faces blurred, deformed by the irregularities in the glass, press up against the window. The carriage lumbers slowly through the crowd. In a flash, I suddenly realize: they've come here to see me, the alleged victim of a rape! The women are observing me with looks of kind compassion which I find ridiculous, the men are leering distrustfully. I recoil back in horror, my father puts his hand on my shoulder to reassure me. I jerk violently away from him. Orazio stares dumbly at his hand as though he were trying to understand why I had been so repelled.

"You have to help me, Misia. I need you. We have to work together to win this case."

I put my hands over my ears and push in very tightly, with the irrepressible urge to start screaming at the top of my lungs like a madwoman. My shoulders are shaking convulsively. I want to vomit, fall asleep, be dead.

🜹

There are almost just as many people inside the courtroom, squeezing on to the long wooden seats, some with picnic baskets on their knees.
One never knows, a little snack just might come in handy in case there
is a dull moment here or there, I think bitterly. My father's friends and
backers form a compact group in the center of the room. Standing there
in full force are all of his colleagues from the via della Croce. Among
them, Giovan Stiattesi, a very good friend of Papa's, the son of the agent
who helped him escape his unhappy childhood. We will be staying at his
home throughout our sojourn in Rome. I am mortified; I would have preferred an anonymous crowd or at least a room without spectators. The
idea that my private life be laid bare to so many people shames me.

An armor-clad soldier with a halberd intimates that I should take a
seat next to my father at the prosecution table. I think, "My true place
is with Agostino!" And yet I comply as though I had no will of my own.

The session opens with the old judge in a black gown reading the
charges. He makes me think of a fat fly buzzing about my ear. I keep
my eyes turned away from Agostino, who is sitting in the dock next to
Cosimo Quorli, the secretary to the Pope. Quorli has come to stand up
for Tassi and he is presently leaning over, whispering in his ear. Agostino
isn't listening to him, I can sense that he is staring at me. Both of these
men are guilty of assaulting me, and yet, though he did not achieve his
ends, it is Cosimo Quorli who deserves to be in my adventurer's place
today. He truly is the most reprehensible of the two. He had no inten-
tion of giving me love!

My father speaks in his turn. His cheeks turning crimson with emotion
as he points a vindictive finger at Agostino. Papa is standing on his tiptoes,
an embarrassing sign of his vulnerability and lack of self-confidence, I
think. I didn't hear the beginning of his complaint, but I happen to catch
this sentence, "An innocent child of fifteen who was his student . . ."

Fifteen? I was still at the convent at fifteen. Why is my father telling
such glaring lies? I know the answer only all too well.

"Not fifteen, seventeen," Agostino interrupts him irritatedly. "Master Gentileschi is being deceitful about his daughter's age in hopes of aggravating my sentence."

What sentence is he speaking of? He won't be condemned. To prison? And we will be separated? For weeks, months, years? I refuse to consider this possibility.

"Was she born in 1593 or in 1595?" asks the scribe, who is recording every word in an enormous red book.

There are huge tufts of hair coming out of the clerk's nostrils and ears. I squint my eyes to distract myself and transform him into a dog, then into a wild boar. How many paintbrushes could I make with all of that hair? One? Two?

Agostino is addressing the judge. He seems to have come to the same conlusion as I have. "Orazio's prime interests are his prestige and his pocketbook," he says. "He hopes to complete the frescoes that the Pope commissioned me to paint, and receive my salary. This man's behavior is dictated by jealousy!"

How right you are, my love. I repeat the words over to myself until they make my head spin, to forget the ugliness, the pettiness, so that I won't have to hear any more. The words echoing through my mind no longer mean anything. Orazio's voice reaches my ears deformed, very loud, as if in a nightmare.

"I ask only one thing, that the damage caused to an honorable name and to my daughter's reputation be atoned for."

Agostino's eyes have just trapped mine. I know, I've gone and let my guard down, but I don't regret it. I'm even angry with myself for not having trusted him more. What had I feared? His disapproval? His rage?

With his eyes lost in mine, he speaks out in a clear, firm voice, a voice filled with tenderness, "Ask Artemisia if I harmed her. I have done nothing, and would never do anything, to hurt her." I want to break down in tears.

At last a glimmer of truth in the midst of all these lies, at last some words of love in this vast flow of hatred. I forgive you, my love, for having not been completely honest in claiming that you never hurt me, for I know that, in your own way, you are sincere. Though you wounded my body in violating my intimacy, you have never once caused pain to my soul, quite the contrary. After having deflowered me, you begged for my forgiveness a thousand times over. You didn't know I was a virgin, you thought that I had already given myself to Fulvio, after you saw my nude sketches of him.

The long white wisps of the judge's beard sweep across the polished oak of the bench. He bangs the gavel down once to quiet the room and, addressing Agostino, states: "You claim that you love this young woman. In that case, why not marry her? You would have your beloved by your side, and Orazio would owe you a dowry. You have everything to win."

Now, it is my lover who avoids my eyes. He looks down and remains strangely silent. Stop torturing him! This concerns me more than anyone else, and I am prepared to accept Agostino's silence, the curiously obstinate objection that he has to the idea of taking me for his wife. A flood of indignation fills me, bringing me out of my torpid silence. I think I've found a way to put an end to this ugly debate.

"You have no right to be putting me up for sale in this way!" I shout at the judge. "I am a virgin and there is no reason for submitting me to this!"

The whole gallery marks an astonished silence. The muscles in the old judge's jaw flinch and he turns toward my father. "In that case, what crime has been committed? The charges will be dismissed," he exclaims with the gavel raised, prepared to call an end to the session.

Orazio lifts his hand to stop the gesture that will adjourn the court, whispering to me at the same time, "Please, don't make things worse for yourself, help me to protect you. I'm only doing this for you."

"The child would say anything to avoid having the pain of appearing in court today added to the suffering that this rape has already caused her."

Impatient, the judge decrees, "The session is suspended until tomorrow."

33

I thought I had done the right thing in claiming that I was a virgin, but I soon learn it was a terrible mistake! As soon as we sit down in the courtroom the following day the old judge calls to one of the guards, "Pull the curtain for the Gentileschi girl!"

The soldier hurries over to draw a large piece of heavy material, undoubtedly set up the day before, across one corner of the room. A curtain? We aren't in my father's studio for a male study in the nude, as far as I know.

Papa, whom I have refused to speak with since yesterday, is looking at me imploringly. "Forgive me, Misia my dear. We are doing this for your own good."

How dare he? And what is that shriveled-up-looking nun followed by the brittle old midwife carrying a basin of water doing here?

Now two men dressed in black are carrying a pair of sawhorses and a wide board—the kind that is used for making coffins—over behind the curtain. The judge orders me to stand, "Mistress Gentileschi, go into the examining room please."

What room? What will be examined?

I walk over to the designated place. The curtain abruptly closes behind me. Now I am alone with the nun and her assistant. The two women definitely do not appear to feel kindly toward me.

"Lie down on the table with your skirt pulled up, your legs spread apart," orders the sister of mercy in a voice so loud that it surely creates a sensation on the far side of the courtroom.

I lie down as I have been told and, to hide my shame, lift my skirts up over my face. My knees are pressed tightly together; I simply cannot open my thighs.

"Spread them wide," an authoritative voice says sharply.

It is the midwife who is talking now. I feel as though I no longer exist, as though I've been annihilated. Better to obey and get this over with as quickly as possible. But still, I would never have expected this kind of brutality. The most tender reaches of my flesh mercilessly wrenched open, the hard woodlike finger, searchingly penetrating my vagina. No sooner has it been withdrawn than an entire hand—fingers in the form of a cone—replaces it. The bony dry hand inspects my intimate regions, dryer still, tearing at my soul as well as at my flesh. Under the horrid onslaught, my dress slips off of my head. I am staring at the woman who is causing me this unbearable pain right in the eye. It is the nun. Her wide-winged coif casts a terrifying shadow on her face. In spite of the air of grave reserve she has assumed, the wife of God— for it is in these terms that women of this sort like to think of themselves—seems to be taking real pleasure in her task as if the divine hand of the Most High itself were proving the wicked deeds of a sinful woman to society.

Now I understand what rape is. True rape. It is not born of an irrepressible desire, does not stem from a loss of control over the senses— no, it comes from the cool conviction of someone who believes they are in the right, and that somehow what they must sanctimoniously accomplish is necessary. Everyone present in the courtroom, on the other side of the curtain, knows the heinous palpation I am being submitted to, and they too, with an ignoble and secret jubilation, must find my tortures necessary as well as appropriate. Only one voice in the room rises in protest: it is Agostino fulminating against the judge, calling him inhumane, almost threatening him, until my bold adventurer and the guards who have run up to neutralize him grapple for a short moment. Then silence falls once again.

The midwife inspects me in turn, just as rudely, she too drawing out her pleasure. And when they have finished their examination, the two old women scrupulously wash their hands in the basin, which had been meant only for that.

I bolt up into a sitting position, revolted. "You wash your hands after having touched me, and not before, as if I were an animal!"

I don't even have time to pull my skirts down before the curtain is abruptly torn open. Perhaps the spectators are taking bets upon whether my virginity has been lost or conserved? I'm certain that almost every man in the room felt his fly bulging at the thought of what was occurring behind the curtain.

A guard guides me back to my seat as the nun and the midwife go to testify in the witness stand. In mute supplication, Agostino casts a desperate glance in my direction, not even trying to hide the hot tears of indignation in his eyes.

Pounding his gavel sharply three times the judge calls for order. "Please! This court demands that common decency be respected!" Then, he turns to the two witnesses. "And so?"

The nun begins first. "I have examined the private parts of the woman known as Artemisia Gentileschi, present in this room, and I declare that she is not a virgin. I am certain of this because when I introduced my finger, I found the maidenhead torn."

My father jumps to his feet. "Just as I said, my daughter was raped by that heathen beast!"

Angry grumblings arise from the crowd. My family's backers encourage them. Someone cries, "Burn the Satan at the stake!"

The judge is compelled to quiet the room once again before addressing the midwife. "Dame Caterina, the court will hear your testimony as well."

What more could be said? It's all over with. As hard as I've tried to claim Agostino's innocence, my father has won in the end, the poor wretch!

"I also investigated the nature of this young woman and, on the strength of my experience, I swear before God that the fault occurred some time ago and is not something recent as the plaintiff claims."

"I never said that he had just recently abused her," my father retorts. "Just imagine the nightmare the poor child must have lived through, having to remain silent and go back to the lessons at her rapist's side. The chaperone told me only yesterday that Artemisia begged her not to leave her for a second, that she seemed terribly frightened of Agostino Tassi. The young woman, whose name is Marisa and who has been in my service since she was a child, simply ascribed it to a proper young woman's natural shyness. She can come to testify if you would like."

Stop lying father, don't destroy the wonderful image I had of you forever. What are you planning to do? Force our little Marisa to damn herself? Make her bear false testimony while swearing upon the Holy Bible that she is telling the truth?

The midwife clears her throat to prepare to speak again. It's obvious she is burning with impatience to continue her report. "Is there anything else you have to add, Dame Caterina?" asks the judge.

"I found the private parts of the Gentileschi girl dilated to the point that there is no doubt that she has already had sexual intercourse on numerous occasions."

"How many occasions?"

Opening and closing both hands three times, the old woman contemptuously lets drop, "At least thirty, if not more." Surprised and indignant murmurs escape from the crowd; the spectators are fidgeting around on the benches, mouths agape, blank-eyed. Orazio blanches and collapses onto his chair.

Several minutes pass before my father says in a weak voice, "So he raped her that many times? The crime is all the more monstrous if it was repeated, and has been repeated for months now!"

"You are making a mockery of justice, Master Gentileschi! You yourself claimed that her chaperone never left her side."

"Perhaps the chaperone was Tassi's accomplice?" my father suggests.

"I did not find any evidence of damaged vaginal tissues," the midwife comments, "which infers that your daughter was, at least of late, fully consenting."

"Or else that she indulged in depravity in the company of other men," the judge suggests. "If there is still a question of rape having been committed, all you have succeeded in proving thus far, Master Gentileschi, is that your daughter is a liar. She claimed she was a virgin, when she isn't in the least!"

The insult strikes my father, more than it does me, like a slap in the face. In any case, being a minor and a woman, therefore doubly inferior, my father represents me in this court and speaks in my name. Never once has anyone questioned me or asked for my opinion. I simply do not exist, nothing that I have to say will really be taken into consideration, and it is why I say nothing and will continue to say nothing till the end.

If I were to tell the simple truth, that Tassi forced me the first time and that we made love thereafter, would he not be pursued for rape anyway? Would I have to wait until he had served his sentence to don my wedding gown . . . ? I don't understand the complexities of the law and I am afraid of making another dreadful mistake trying to be canny. Yes, it's better just to keep quiet, to hope for a miracle.

Agostino seems to be suddenly stricken with the same listless inactivity as I am. As if he too were putting his life, our life, into the hands of fate. What could we possibly hope for? That the judge and the whole assembly should grow so tired of our muteness that they would annul the entire trial? That it all somehow just turns out to be a bad dream?

We are allowing ourselves to be manipulated like two pawns on a gameboard, and yet it would only take one word from Agostino to bring our torments to an end. He could simply swear on the Holy Bible to have always taken me with my full consent and promise to marry me. It is up to him to tell this lie, for he is more at fault than I am. If one of us must be damned, it is only fair that it be Agostino. What crazy thoughts! My faith in the Almighty is too great for me to bear having the man I love banished from Paradise. Isn't it worse to be condemned to Hell than to prison? My lover and I are caught in an endless circle, there is no way out. On the one hand we cannot lie, and yet neither can we tell the truth.

I can see from the look on his face, from his attitude, that Cosimo Quorli has come upon some sort of solution. He has been quite agitated for some time now, casting mean looks in my direction and gloating all the while. I suppose that he hopes to throw all the blame onto me in order to absolve Agostino. By what means? I do not know, but I am sorry that a man as wonderful as my adventurer chooses his friends so poorly. Cosimo Quorli is a destructive person and the only reason I didn't tell Agostino about his attacking me was because I didn't want him to have to part with such an influential patron. My own entourage is no better. My father may get on his high horse in my defense if he likes, but this trial is all his fault. Moreover, he's proven himself to be a barefaced liar, which has destroyed the very foundations of the confidence I had in him. I have lost all respect for him. Fortunately none of his testimony was given under oath! I am nevertheless convinced that he would be quite capable of committing perjury just to carry his revenge out to the bitter end.

34

Day four of the trial. Just a minute ago, a small, weasel-faced man came up and stood behind Agostino and Cosimo Quorli. Laying his hand on Agostino's shoulder, he introduces himself to the court. "My name is Paolo Lombardo, attorney for the accused."

Agostino jumps to his feet seething with indignation. "An attorney? I don't need an attorney!"

"It is required by law," responds the judge. "You have the right to stand in your own defense but, as you seem to wish to remain stubbornly silent, someone had to be appointed to represent you. The court can not sustain an objection on your part at this late date. Rather, you should thank your kind patron, Cosimo Quorli, for having engaged the best lawyer in the city."

Agostino protests, but the arguments of the assigned defense attorney finally persuade him, and he grudgingly concedes.

"Bring in the witness!" calls the judge, motioning to a guard posted at the door.

The courtroom begins to buzz excitedly as Costanza makes a striking entrance in a flamenco dress with bright yellow flounces. She walks impassively to the bench past the male spectators who gawk at her greedily.

My father springs out to meet her as if he wishes to keep her from speaking. "Just how long have you been Agostino Tassi's sister? Eh?"

"I do not understand your question," Costanza replies, shrugging her shoulders.

"Must I repeat everything I've learned about you?"

"Return to your seat, Gentileschi," orders the old judge. Then, turning toward the attorney, he says, "It is your witness, Counsel."

"Oh, I have only one question. Mistress Costanza, what is your opinion of the accused?"

With one finger, the beautiful courtesan sensually caresses the wooden railing upon which she is leaning. And, in an extremely unusual voice, whose inflections are almost erotic, she says, "I've known Agostino for years. I was his mistress . . . a mistress he did not love. He never promised me anything. In fact, one could say that he ended up honoring this non-promise when he left me. In any case, I can testify to the fact that Agostino is incapable of raping anyone. He has always shown himself to be particularly attentive to procuring pleasure for women."

A nostalgic sigh raises her voluptuous breast.

"I beg you not to forget you are in a court of law!" growls the judge.

Costanza goes on, now despondently. "After he met Artemisia, I watched him slowly change as the days went by. I would give anything to have him look at me in the way he does her. She is, in my opinion, the first woman that he has ever really loved."

"You are a prostitute, a professional in the service of pleasure seeking!" my father says contemptuously. "It is indecent to hear you speaking of love."

"Master Gentileschi! You are speaking entirely out of turn!" chides the magistrate.

The lawyer smiles at Costanza with satisfaction, saying, "Thank you for being so frank. You may retire."

Before leaving the courtroom, Costanza casts an ambiguous look at me—a mixture of admiration and reproach—as if at one and the same time she were saluting my ability to awaken such passion in the man that she still loved, and holding me responsible for Agostino's current dilemma. She obviously believes I helped my father trump up this whole story of rape. So she thinks I'm Orazio's ally? Yet it seems to me that Costanza would be able to see into my soul, if only because we are both in love with the same man. Cosimo Quorli and the lawyer undoubtedly got her agreement to testify against me by playing on the jealousy that she must surely feel.

The young rhetorician fills the space intelligently; he springs to the right, bounds to the left, grows rigid with exasperation, pales, blushes, raises his fist theatrically, in other words, gets the most out of the tiny amount of room he has at his disposal. He does so well that one hundred pairs of wide eyes are riveted upon him. The spectators are left gaping in open-mouthed admiration.

It's true that all this vigorous self-confidence makes one's head swim. The public must think that since this man is exerting himself to this extent, he is certainly in the right. I must recall the stances he takes and use them in the scenic organization of my future paintings. How truly incorrigible I am, my mind is always straying! *Come back to earth, Artemisia, get your feet on the ground!* It's not that I'm indifferent or uninterested in my fate or that of Agostino, it's just that I don't want to suffer anymore. I have always been guided by a wonderful instinct for happiness that now refuses to be tyrannized by this whole abomination. I find myself thinking, *This isn't where I belong, I belong in the arms of my adventurer.*

Yet the voice of reason cackles within me: *Wake up, girl! It's every man for himself now. Agostino hasn't lifted a finger to get you out of this mess, no one is even mentioning marriage anymore, and his attorney is out to get you. Who is there to stand up for you? A father whose interests are in direct conflict with yours? There's no one else. The tables are being turned, watch your step!*

I protest lamely: *That lawyer doesn't even know me, I never did him any harm, I'm innocent...*

The same implacable voice of reason responds: *Little matter, justice is not always triumphant on this earth, that's just the way it is. The attorney is simply doing his job!*

As a matter of fact, the virtuoso at the bar is demonstrating his ingenuity once again. There he is brandishing the notorious green portfolio that, for months, never left my side, yet I foolishly left it at

Agostino's house. He takes out a pile of sketches, the worst ones, those inspired by Fulvio's charming anatomy. Waving them under the nose of the stunned spectators, he proclaims, "Gentlemen, I beg you to examine these, ladies please turn your eyes away! This is how Artemisia Gentileschi spends her days. Drawing the virile organs of men, and her father dares to assert that she is chaste! Just observe the precision of the lines, the emotion in the detail. These are, without a doubt, souvenirs she was keeping of her various lovers. For, as you can see for yourselves, the graceful adolescent torso and limbs depicted here could in no way belong to my client." My father stares at me in surprise and consternation. His bottom lip quivers in rhythm with the trembling of the rest of his body. I sense that he is shaken, devastated, ready to admit defeat.

"In any case," continues the attorney, "these sketches are sure proof that Artmisia Gentileschi has an in-depth knowledge of the ways of the flesh."

Then, turning toward the judge, he adds, "Yes, Your Honor, I too am of your opinion! As you do, I consider Artemisia guilty of a double crime, and therefore it is only fair that she be doubly punished. She claims to have been raped, yet why should she have refused her favors to the handsome Agostino Tassi more fervently than she does to anyone else? Would this not seem illogical?"

He takes a few more strides in front of the bench to give everyone the time to digest this "obvious fact."

"And, on top of everything," he resumes, "Artemisia violated the Divine Law as decreed by His Holiness, the Pope. Yes, herein lies the true rape! I needn't remind anyone that it is strictly forbidden for women to study and represent masculine anatomy. This young woman did not simply circumvent the edict in sketching a shoulder or a bust, which would have been inadmissible in itself, she pushed her vice to the point of describing with her crayon those parts of the body that God himself wishes to be veiled. Did He not, in the beginnings of mankind, recommend that Adam and Eve cover their private parts with a fig leaf?"

A deep rumble drifts from the spectators who are considering me disapprovingly; suddenly, father's face brightens with a faint ray of hope. "It is I who did those studies. It is a perfectly acceptable activity for a painter to engage in, isn't it? As my model, I used a young fisherman, known by the name of Fulvio, who lives in our village. I will ask him to come and bear witness tomorrow."

You hit it right on the head, Father, the drawings are of Fulvio all right. I thought for a second that you had learned about the cave, but the truth is even more sordid. You know that Fulvio has always been in love with me and that you won't have any trouble persuading him to commit perjury to defend me.

"He's lying!" exclaims the attorney in livid exultation. "This isn't the work of a painter, it is the work of a woman. Look at the signature, Artemisia . . . Artemisia . . . here too, Artemisia."

The gallery is in an uproar. "What a family! A liar and a harlot!"

"This trial is a sham!"

"Release Tassi!"

"Tassi is innocent!"

My father hides his face in his cap, ashamed at having been caught in a flagrant lie. As for myself, I regret having ever signed those drawings. It's not really that I was proud of them, it's just that my name is the only word I know how to write.

At a sign from the lawyer, Batisto, Tassi's assistant, walks up to the bar with a rolled canvas in his hand. Whatever will they come up with next? The attorney unrolls the canvas with a snap and, holding it out between his thumb and forefinger in utter disgust, he exhibits it as if it were some monster in a side show. It's my *Judith and Holofernes!*

"See for yourselves!" he cries. "She claims to be virtuous, and this is what she paints! Look at the effusion of blood in this painting. If two women had wished to slit a pig's throat, they wouldn't have gone about it any differently."

I don't see what that has to do with anything. What wrong is there in having represented the famous myth of Judith? What will he invent now? I'm absolutely confident he'll find something . . .

Momentarily forgetting where I am, I become the apprentice painter once again, the novice anxious to know my father's opinion of my work, I shoot a furtive glimpse at him. He, too, seems to be somehow absent. He has stood up, his eyes are riveted on the painting; in spite of himself, his whole face is expressing admiration and pride. It only lasts a fraction of a second, but it warms my heart. The magical moment comes to an end when the attorney resumes his case.

"As we can all see, this is a painting of Judith decapitating Holofernes. Judith and her servant have overwhelmed the Assyrian general who is attempting to defend himself in vain. The sword cuts into the neck, the blood spurts out. It is clear that Artemisia has lent her own features to Judith, and those of Agostino Tassi to Holofernes. As for the servant, I have confirmed my first intuition. It is, of course, Marisa, the alleged chaperone."

He points a grotesquely theatrical and terrifyingly vicious finger in my direction. "Artemisia even sees herself as a Judith, a perfidious criminal . . . and Agostino . . ." The attorney abruptly turns the canvas so that Holofernes, whom I had painted lying on his back, is now in a vertical position. "And Agostino," he pursues, "as a victim of her machinations! Artemisia and Agostino, who is the victim of whom?"

This time the crowd reacts with even more hostility toward me. The terrible violence unleashed against me has my mind in a whirl. I shake my head to fight the off dizziness. It will all stop soon, it just can't continue. And yet . . .

"Judith—Artemisia, I mean to say—seduced her victim. She gained his confidence by means of her feminine wiles, she put him under a spell, exactly as a witch would." And, designating Agostino sitting stiffly on his seat, as if petrified, the attorney exclaims, "There the poor man sits, completely subjugated, thinking an innocent sleep is overtaking him when Artemisia wants only one thing, to cut his throat."

Here, to enhance the dramatic effect, the orator carefully pauses before enjoining the judge in a voice booming with emotion. "Your honor, do you wish to serve as Artemisia's glaive?"

He paces up and down once again—this is obviously one of his oratory techniques—then turns to my lover. "And you, Agostino Tassi, will you not stand up at last and claim your innocence before it is too late . . . ?"

The last remark has an odd ring to it, lacking in conviction, sincerity. All of a sudden I realize that neither the attorney nor Cosimo Quorli really want Agostino to speak. Just a little while ago, when everything seemed so overwhelming and I thought I was going to faint, my adventurer had given a start. Although I was too preoccupied to pay much attention at the time, now his reaction comes back to me ever more clearly. First, the anxious look, his eyes clinging to mine which were beginning to roll backward, then his face contorted with a mixture of compassion, remorse, determination. I recall him putting his hand on his seat in order to stand, the look of sacrifice that his features took on in that instant, his lips which opened to cry out the truth, to finally end my torture. This time he will rise up so very tall and begin to speak, he will dispel all of the horrid thoughts besieging me . . . but no! Just as before, Cosimo Quorli grabs him by the arm and forces him to remain seated, murmuring a few words in his ear. And as before, Agostino concedes, sits back down with a pained face and is still. I wonder what Quorli says to him, what are the words that have so much power over him . . . ? Anyway, what had my lover decided to declare? He hadn't simply intended to admit to the rape, I am certain of that. He seemed altogether too devastated for that. Something is eluding me.

35

The judge is attending the funeral of a close family member, and he will not be back for a week. Agostino and I have been granted a reprieve before the torture recommences. I was relieved to leave Giovan Stiattesi's residence and reach my beloved village after four hours of bumpy roads.

As soon as we are home, the first thing I want to do is to go and confess to Father Anselmo who, over and above his duty as a priest, is a good and open-minded man. I tell him everything in detail. The words flow steadily from my lips, as though they had long ago formed a row of brave little soldiers prepared to charge. As I go further into the story, the frustration I had kept pent-up for so long is released, and I become increasingly relaxed. Finally, a feeling of serenity spreads over me. At last I can tell the truth! Father Anselmo first listens to me without intervening, and then, before I leave the confessional, forgetting to give me my penance, he advises me to strongly urge Agostino to plead guilty.

"If rape is followed by marriage, it is not a punishable crime."

"Are you absolutely certain?" I say in a choked voice, clinging to the wooden latticework that separates us. "Why didn't the judge mention it then?"

Father Anselmo laughs heartily. "For the simple reason that ignorance of the law is no excuse. It is not your judge's vocation to allow crimes go unpunished, especially since this particular clause has been the source of much abuse. Too often, poor victims are forced to marry their rapists so as to quiet the rumormongers and conclude the matter to everyone's satisfaction. But this is not the case with you. You love him and he feels the same way about you. Go now in peace, my child and good luck!"

I want to clap my hands with glee. So, everything might just work out happily in the end! I leave the church elated and full of hope, wondering how I might inform Agostino of my discovery. But there is no way, since I have neither the means to get back to Rome nor the money to bribe a prison guard. I cannot send him a letter either. Whom could I trust to write and deliver it? The old priest would surely refuse, for fear of compromising himself. As for my father, his thirst for revenge against Tassi is too great. And anyway, as if to spare me a terrible confrontation, he disappeared from the village as soon as we arrived.

In fact, the week goes by without our hearing a word from Orazio. Where can he have gone? Tuzia simply arches her brows enigmatically in response to my questions. It also seems odd to me that Tassi wasn't informed by his attorney about this particular provision in the law. He surely must know about the miraculous clause. Why then hadn't he advised his client to marry?

Once again, I am racked with doubt and anxiety. Then suddenly, the obvious answer dawns upon me: the attorney works first and foremost for Cosimo Quorli, and only secondly for Agostino. Moreover, judging from the virulent looks the secretary to the Pope is always giving me, I can only conclude that he never swallowed having his designs on me thwarted in the pine forest, or my kneeing him between the legs, so he is out to destroy me. That is why his attorney is dragging me through the mud like this. Quorli is killing two birds with one stone: proving his friend innocent and taking vengeance on me to boot.

36

Acting very secretively and appearing to be quite satisfied with himself, Orazio has come back to take me to court. He looks both exhausted and rejuvenated after his weeklong escapade. I wouldn't have held it against him if he'd never come back.

We won't be taking the usual hired carriage. Instead, we seat ourselves in a coach equipped with two separate compartments, and one extra horse. In the front compartment sits a dark shape, covered with a tulle veil. I ask my father who the person on the other side of the partition is. He turns his back and pretends to be asleep.

In the courtroom, the session opens with a reiteration of the court proceedings that the hirsute clerk rattles off mechanically. Listening to him, I suddenly realize that the situation has changed drastically. The attorney has turned the whole case around in Agostino's favor. Soon it will be me they'll be throwing into prison. It sounds as if my father and I were plotting against Master Tassi, and that in addition to being a painter, which is not fitting for a woman, I am also depraved. To avoid the hostile looks coming from the spectators and the obviously exasperated judge, who makes no secret of his distrust of me, I begin, obsessively, to make little drawings on a couple of sheets of paper that I have brought with me this morning. I sketch the attorney, the clerk, Cosimo Quorli, a guard, some of the spectators. Once again, drawing helps me to withdraw from the world, retire within myself. In one corner of the paper, which is now completely covered, I draw the emaciated face of Agostino who, I just noticed, is sketching just as I am, lifting his eyes from the paper only long enough to stare at me intensely. What is he trying to tell me? I am drawing him, he is drawing me: we are making love through these lines.

I am also desperately trying to think of a way of communicating with my adventurer without anyone knowing. How can I inform him of what the priest told me? Though I can't have a written message passed to him, maybe I can scrawl out some kind of picture that would make him understand that if he confesses to the rape and swears to marry me, he will not be prosecuted.

As I am thinking about how to accomplish this, a strange woman is ushered into the courtroom. The black dress, the heavy veil hiding her face, it must be the silhouette, the mysterious passenger who rode in our coach.

The apparition walks toward me and whispers in my ear, "My poor child, the man you hold dear to your heart has sown misfortune in his path since his earliest childhood." Then it walks toward the witness box and stands there before the astonished gallery without saying a word. Only then does my father rise to address the court. His voice is so vibrant with self-satisfaction that I fear the worst.

"I would like to introduce my witness to the court," he begins.

The woman slowly raises the veil uncovering a severe, middle-aged face.

You would think that Agostino had seen a ghost. The blood leaves his face as he bounds to his feet as if on a spring. His crayon breaks in his enraged fist. "What are you doing here?" he rails.

The stranger looks at him with a disdainful pout, and turns back to the bench.

"Ladies and Gentlemen, the woman you have before your eyes is Agostino Tassi's legitimate wife!" my father cries in triumph.

A surprised murmur rises from one hundred throats, filling the room. As for me, I am in the grips of a paroxysm of shock. My head is absolutely empty, an icy sweat breaks out all over my body. The cold runs down to my shoulders, enters my backbone. My palms are moist, the light is flashing, I can't breathe, my knees are weak, and my heart is racing. Am I going to die? I wish I could faint, to escape from this hell. I would be willing to accept never waking up again. I just want this terrible feeling to stop immediately.

My father's words reach my ears deformed, booming, choppy. He is speaking in the name of this woman, just as he did for me before. "I found it odd that Agostino obstinately declined to marry my daughter. I spent a week in Florence investigating the matter. Very few people were aware of this marriage. . . . Yet here she is, the poor wife, rejected, despoiled, abandoned."

"She left me of her own free will!" Agostino protests. "This is a masquerade!"

My left eyelid has begun to twitch uncontrollably. I need some air! Some air! I'm suffocating!

"Would you like proof of what I'm saying?" Orazio pursues. "Here is the marriage certificate. Agostino Tassi married Aureliana Dipoli, present in this room, in a small church near Florence and, without even taking time to give her a child, he ran away with one of this woman's, his very own wife's, younger sisters."

Then, glaring at me, he adds, "And this is the man you wish to protect?"

Upturning the defendant table, pushing away the guards that try to hold him back, Agostino runs to me.

"Don't believe this nonsense, Artemisia!"

He strives to explain to me that the marriage had been error of his youth, that he had separated from his wife on friendly terms, that he had left Florence alone.

I can't hear him at all. There is a loud buzzing in my ears, the words are drowned out in a sort of dense fog. I no longer know where I am. Why is that woman smiling victoriously? Oh, I can tell by the way she acts that she never loved my adventurer. She remains standing there in silence, draped in her dignity, as befits a respectable woman. The judge is an idiot, he ought to be able to see this is one of my father's schemes, that Agostino is telling the truth. I know it is the truth, even if I can't seem to hear what he is saying. Someone tears us away from each other, the guards finally subdue him and force him to go back to his seat as the judge pounds away with his gavel. The session is suspended until late in the afternoon.

I just sit there, almost lifeless, incapable of getting my breath back. The piece of paper I was drawing on falls to the floor. The boorish clerk picks it up. What is he saying? He is smiling hideously, trying to slip something into my hand.

"A piece of gold for your drawing . . . Sign it for me, I beg you."

I push the scribe away, tear up my drawing, and walk to the door as if I were a sleepwalker, with arms stretched out in front of me.

Then suddenly the room turns upside down, I fall heavily to the floor, everything goes black.

37

I regain consciousness in the small room that I occupy in the home of my father's friend, Giovan Stiattesi, and gloomily contemplate the child's toys that are neatly arranged in one corner, the little pine dressing table, the pretty little set of toilet articles that have decorated it, untouched, for years. With a dejected finger I lift the lid of the basketwork chest sitting on the night stand, filled with the kind of baubles that little girls find so precious. Minerva, whose room I've been given, was approximately my age when she was carried away with an illness. Ominously blond and pale, of a spectral beauty that delighted her father, Minerva was never really a part of this world. Every night, our host creeps into the room and watches me sleep. He pulls the blanket gently over my shoulders, I hear him murmur, "Good night, Minerva," before he tiptoes away.

Sitting cross-legged on the dead girl's narrow bed, I am trying to get used to the idea that, since the Church forbids divorce, and Agostino is already married, I will have to give him up. It might seem simple to say, but it sticks in my throat. God knows how I love him, my adventurer, even despite his betrayal! Why didn't he ever tell me he was married? Things could have been a lot simpler. As a virtuous girl, I would have renounced ever having the man and satisfied myself with the professor. Or else, as an immoral girl, which I am in a way, I would have become his mistress, but knowing full well where I stood. His lying to me has made all of my dreams, all of my illusions come crashing down around my feet all at once. I could weep, cry out in rage, but no, I do nothing of the sort. With cold lucidity, I stow my feelings away in a far corner of my heart. Why continue to fight when I have no arms with which to defend myself? Only one thing matters to me now: seeing Agostino alone.

Working from memory, I trace the portrait of the court clerk. Elongated snout, bushy eyebrows . . . I draw in less hair and make him more charismatic. I have to be able to depict him in such a way that he will recognize himself and also feel flattered. After two false starts, I've got it. I believe the drawing will please him. At the bottom of the page, I add a very legible signature.

He wanted a drawing, so he'll have one. I don't believe for an instant that the man is interested in art. Rather, he's caught scent of a lucrative deal. A little portrait drawn by the hand of the woman responsible for this whole scandal will probably fetch a handsome price. And who knows? What if I became truly famous one day . . . ?

With a light mantilla over my shoulders, I run through the icy wind to the Court of Justice. "What clerk?" asks the guard on duty. "There are several clerks here." I show him my drawing. "Ah! Sandrone di Pietro! You'll find him on the first floor, next to the last door on the right." There is hardly anyone in the old building at this time of night. I knock.

The man looks at my sketch as if he were examining himself in a mirror. He nods his head appreciatively. "Have you changed your mind, then?" he asks.

"No, sir. I'm not interested in your gold florin, but the drawing will be yours if you succeed in getting me into Agostino Tassi's cell. I wish to speak with him alone."

It doesn't take long to convince the clerk. He leads me down a ghastly flight of stairs between two thick walls, sweating with humidity. A small negotiation with the jailer, a silver coin changes hands this time. There must not be many visitors here. The prisoners use my presence to vent the sexual privations inflicted upon them. I don't really mind.

At the other end of the passage we reach a thick wooden door. "You have ten minutes, no longer," the jailer warns before turning the key in the lock.

A large chandelier lights the room. Due to his influential friends, my adventurer is accorded special treatment. A cot with a crucifix hanging over it, a table, and two wicker chairs furnish the vaulted room in which he has been imprisoned. He must have his meals sent in from outside. A plate of mutton stew—untouched—is growing cold before a carafe of wine.

Agostino is lying on the bed. He lifts himself up on one elbow and watches me come forward in the wavering light of the candles. His sad smile lights my heart. "Is it you?" he asks incredulously.

"It's me."

We could remain like this, completely still, our eyes locked together, for eternity. The most important thing has been said, but I must know more: Agostino owes me an explanation. I want to know the truth about everything.

"Why did you keep the fact that you were married a secret from me?" I demand.

"So that I wouldn't lose you. I would have done anything in the world to keep you with me. Your father is to blame for our unhappiness."

Coldly, I remark, "My father isn't responsible for your past."

"Forgive me, my love, forgive me for all of the pain that has been inflicted upon you. I would like to strangle them, all of the swine that feed off your suffering."

"In the meantime," I comment snidely, "I imagine they are all snoring happily, that they will awaken tomorrow with a smile on their lips, terribly impatient for the quarry to be blown again at the Court of Justice."

"Artemisia, if there was any way I could have married you, I swear I wouldn't have needed a Court of Justice to force me to do so."

I am torn between wanting to slap him and the urge to jump into his arms. So it's true that he loves me? That he would have wanted me for his wife? I glower at him, "You allowed your attorney to drag me through the mud. You're the only one who knew where my portfolio full of drawings was hidden."

"Yes, it was even my idea to use it as a piece of evidence in the trial," he admits.

"You can't be serious!"

"We had worked out a plan. Cosimo knew that I had a wife in Florence," Agostino explains.

Feeling suddenly ashamed, I snap, "Oh, so he knew about it, did he? How many other people were in on it? What a silly fool I must have seemed!"

Agostino stares at me remorsefully. "Calm down. Of course Cosimo knew my wife, we've been friends for over twenty years. But she and I never loved each other. Aureliana lived with her parents, in her native village, whereas I lived in Florence. Very few people had been told the secret. The law is such that if I were to have admitted having been married to Aureliana, I would have been immediately convicted of adultery and imprisoned. That would have been the end of the story."

"Yet we're precisely at that same point now," I remark bitterly.

A long silence ensues, he doesn't know what to say anymore. He and I were made for embraces and laughter, not for pathos and blame. He asks me once again to forgive him for the nightmare he has put me through.

"Are you all right at least? Tell me that you are all right, that you're strong enough to overcome these trials," he says, putting his hands on my shoulders, squeezing my arms, running his palms down my back.

He caresses my hair. The sudden closeness of our bodies, despite the rage and pain that are overwhelming me, makes it impossible for me to push him away. I wish everything could be left just as it is, that I could leave quickly, keeping this feeling within me, and never look back. But, in order to leave him, I must first forgive him. In order to forgive him, if indeed it is possible, I must know.

In a resigned, barely audible voice, I say, "Tell me."

Agostino begins, "The attorney hoped to have the charges dismissed so that . . ."

I stand, my cheeks are hot with anger, "Dismiss the charges?"

"Let me finish, will you?" scolds Tassi.

"Yes," I reply in a childlike voice.

"If the charges had been dismissed in this case, and that could only happen if you were made to look like a brazen and shameless woman, Cosimo Quorli would have been able to file a petition in my favor with the Pope. By an exceptional act, my marriage would have been annulled. I have no children with Aureliana, and I would have claimed that the union was never consummated. Afterward, you and I could have slipped away somewhere until the whole scandal had been forgotten. Finally free from all bonds, I would have tried to make everything up to you by being the best and the most faithful of husbands."

As he pronounces these last words, his face takes on a little melancholy look that would have touched me in other circumstances. "We would have had many children, and lived happily ever after," I conclude sarcastically.

In a hurt voice, he answers, "I don't know how Cosimo ever convinced me of this fine fairy tale. I just ask you to believe me, Artemisia."

"I'm only defending myself. It might have been a good idea! But you should have at least explained it to me! I would have talked to my father, he wouldn't have brought your wife to the witness stand and—"

"You know very well that nothing could have stopped him. He's out for my head."

"You should never have done this, you should have trusted me," I murmur clinging to him more tightly. "What will happen now?"

"Oh, my sweet little thing! Cherished little love of my life . . . ," he says, taking me in his arms, rocking me.

And we remain there, enlaced in silence. Agostino once told me that the way we see things, how we physically describe them, more directly reveals our soul than lengthy perorations. I ask him to depict what he sees from his prison window, beyond the rusty bars. He understands immediately and takes my hands. We close our eyes. His magician's voice carries us away, far away, just as it had when we first met.

"I see two hills, one straddling the other," he says. "In the mornings, a gentle wind lays the thick and tender green grasses down in the same direction, the two small mounts seem to melt into each other and make only one."

"That is the way we were," I murmur.

"But come evening, after having been rumpled and ill-treated by opposing winds, the grasses are frightened and bristly, the hills seem distinct from each other. Vying elements have separated them and they wait despondently, longing to be united once again under the same mantle of green."

"Will they ever be?" I ask in a trembling voice.

"Sometimes, when the moon is full, there is a magic hour of the night when all of nature is bathed in a heavenly light, a light so white that it is impossible to paint with our earthly colors. And yes, on those nights, my two hilltops come secretly together and they blend so utterly with each other that one would think it were impossible to ever separate them again."

"I love you, Agostino."

38

Here we are back in this huge, austere, noisy, ill-lit room again. I feel as though I've been here for months on end, the blessed carefree days of childhood seem so very far away now. The heat is like an oven. Women are fanning themselves, men have taken out their handkerchiefs. Not to weep over the fate of two lovers that have been torn apart, simply to wipe the sweat dripping from their faces.

Some stragglers are quarreling over the few remaining seats. Now there is standing room only. There are even clusters of faces swarming about the windows, hoping to catch every last second of the end of the trial. Some people whisper that the magistrate is finally going to pass judgment, others say he is not ready yet, and that dealing with a couple of dirty pigs such as us, will undoubtedly lead to new and exciting developments. A fat peasant woman with a basketful of eggs under her arm spat on my shoe as I passed. Agostino was treated no better; if it hadn't been for the guards he would undoubtedly have gotten involved in several tussles. The crowd hurls its scornful invectives at me just as mercilessly as it does at him. "Throw the depraved harlot in the hole!" "Death to the adulterer!" "Lock them both up in the same cell, they'll keep each other company!" Jeers and insults echo through the room.

The courtroom is in this state of general agitation when the judge makes his entrance. In effect, he does not seem to have made up his mind yet. Slowly cracking his finger joints one after the other, he first studies Agostino and then me. The look in his eyes vacillates between perplexity and contempt. On the one hand, a young woman of very loose morals, on the other, a philanderer who has the gall to decorate our churches while he wallows in the most grievous venery . . . How to decide?

My father chooses this moment to stand, interrupting in the most irksome fashion the old magistrate's meditation. Orazio apparently deems it necessary to add the finishing touches to his brilliant performance of yesterday. "Therefore, Your Honor," he begins, "since my daughter was in fact raped . . ."

A disturbing gleam lights the judge's eye. I could swear that my father just gave him the idea of how to conclude this matter. He raises his hand to silence the plaintiff. In a voice filled with renewed resolution, he declares, "That is precisely the problem, Master Gentileschi. We are faced with judging a case of rape, and yet the rape has yet to be proven. Now, if God wills, the court intends to prove or disprove this alleged crime. I hereby ordain—"

What could it be that he is debating, to leave his words suspended like this for a long second as if he were thinking it over one last time before committing himself any further?

"I hereby ordain," he finally continues, "that the common question be applied, in camera, to aid in determining the exact responsibilities and faults of each party. So be it!"

Dear God, what does all that gibberish mean? The legal terms that the judge spouted off have sent the whole room into an uproar—what could their meaning be?

Agostino and I are going down a stone staircase, each of us flanked by two armed guards, into the bowels of the building, with steps that grow increasingly humid and slippery as we descend. Where are we going? What is this new test they are going to put us to, a test so secret that they must take us underground to conduct it? Maybe they'll throw us in the dungeons—for how long? All of the questions that are assailing me do not even seem to occur to Agostino. He is moving along with firm, regular steps, as if he was not in the least worried about what was to become of him. Or rather, as if he knew perfectly well what awaited him, and had resigned himself to it. In the glow of the torchlight, a golden halo appears to be framing my adventurer's head. He reminds me of Fra Angelico's paintings of saints walking calmly to their martyrdom. His foot never falters on the moss that grows in scattered patches on the stone steps. Yet, despite the firm hold he keeps on the railing, the old judge preceding us, slips. Agostino catches his fall just as the old balding head was to be cracked open on a sharp corner of stone. Rather than thank him, the magistrate pulls away with disgust. My lover shudders. I think he has just understood to what extent the judge, far from showing any gratitude, will be merciless toward him. Nevertheless his face resumes the same serene expression and, seized by a sudden flash of intuition, I finally realize what that expression is hiding. Agostino is preparing himself for the worst—physical pain. They are going to torture him! That's it, they're taking us to the torture chamber! The abominable butcher, with his blood-spattered leather apron, will torment his body, pierce the flesh I love with white-hot irons, tie his limbs to the wheel, and turn the crank until they are disjointed. And I will have to watch it all? No, never. Before they even touch him, I'll swear that Agostino never raped me, that my father and I had plotted the whole thing, hoping to walk away with the commission for the frescoes. One never knows, I might just be able to convince him. If not, if lying will get me nowhere, he will order the butcher to finish the sinister task. Only then, when the glowing iron is nearing my adventurer's lovely eyes, will I tell the truth, the initial rape, and then all of the love that followed. In any case, Agostino won't crack, he would rather die a thousand deaths in silence than be dishonored in front of me. The "common question," which I had taken to be a private interrogation, is in truth a euphemism, a hypocritical term meaning torture. That is why my father looked so satisfied when the guards grabbed my lover. The butcher is going to make Agostino pay for his crimes in blood. Orazio's hatred is so intense that he must think it fitting for his daughter to witness the punishment. Since my eyes are, in a way, also his, he hopes that through them he will see his slighted honor avenged. In any event, he did absolutely nothing to keep the two helmeted men from pulling me along after Agostino.

This can't be a torture chamber. Contrary to my fears, the terrifying flight of stairs takes us to a small cozy room. The walls are covered in a rich, burgundy-colored velvet and a large silver crucifix—after the Cellini manner—is stuck up on one of them, two others display brackets, silver as well, in which numerous tapers are burning. A bench, several armchairs, a table, and an ebony sideboard inlaid in ivory complete the furnishings. Instead of the monstrous instruments I was expecting to see, a porcelain vase filled with fresh flowers decorates the table. A woolen carpet, as thick as turf and extremely soft underfoot, is spread over the flagstones. You would think it were a private chamber that the judge had reserved for himself, where he liked to come in order to reflect on matters between two sessions. Or perhaps a little love nest in which, despite his great age, he would receive his mistresses, or *filles de joie*.

As the judge is seating himself in one of the armchairs, three of the guards take up their post along the wall. The fourth goes back up the stairs. I can hear the pounding of his heavy boots slowly dying away.

At first, the magistrate seems to be lost in thought. A few minutes later, he points out two other chairs and invites us to sit down. I take my seat very cautiously as if a sharp spring might suddenly poke me. No, the chair is comfortable, quite pleasant. With my hands on my knees, I wait to see what will happen next, initially feeling quite tense, but soon growing more confident. This place is so reassuring, especially since our host seems to be on the verge of going to sleep. His eyes are closed, his head is nodding forward. Is he really sleeping?

Footsteps can be heard once again on the stairs. The old man lifts his chin, the severe expression returns to his face. The fourth guard reappears in the company of the court clerk and a short, middle-aged man with a large belly and a debonair smile. He is the exact image of what one would imagine an assistant clerk to be, with the elbows of his pourpoint worn threadbare. I suppose these two have come to take down our confessions. Yes, that must be it, the judge prefers to interrogate us in front of a limited audience so that we will neither be influenced by our friends nor our foes.

The man I take for the clerk's assistant, rummages around in a pigskin sack and instead of the inkwell and the register that I anticipated, takes out a ball of red cloth with a cord wrapped around it. He struggles with the knots, sticking his tongue out of the corner of his mouth childishly, and looks at us arching his brows and shrugging his shoulders as if to excuse himself for his clumsiness. He finally finishes the task and with the cord in one hand and the ball of red cloth in the other, he walks over to Agostino. It is difficult to keep from laughing out loud, his gait is so ludicrous.

The man unrolls the ball of red cloth. It is a simple apron—inoffensive, in spite of its blood-red color. But the way Agostino flinches uncontrollably fills me with terror. He cannot keep himself from recoiling in his seat, his hands tightly grasping the arms of the chair. He stands up bravely, as white as a sheet, so that the man may put the apron on him, looking at me all the while with an expression of utter devotion.

"No, no," says the judge pointing to me, "first the Gentileschi girl. This case has drawn out long enough, things will go much more quickly with the young lady."

The man gasps and repeats dubiously, "The girl first, Your Honor?"

"The truth. We are going to get to the truth. Apart from the two of you, God only knows the real truth. Stand up Artemisia Gentileschi!"

On trembling knees, I rise, and have the red apron tied around my waist. Agostino cries out, tries to stand between me and the little man, but the four guards quickly subdue him. "Put your hands together," says the man who will torture me, for he is in fact a torturer. "Put your hands together, I tell you! As if you were praying."

"Yes, that's it," says the judge grimly, "pretend, you are well versed in the art!"

As the torturer winds the cord around each of my fingers at the first joint, to separate them from one another, I address a prayer to the Most High and All Merciful, *Have pity on me, please give me the strength to remain silent.*

The judge is still seated in his chair. With his fist in his cheek, he asks me, "Did Agostino Tassi rape you?"

I don't answer, my eyes are riveted to those of my lover, who is screaming at me to tell the truth. A guard strikes him on the head with the pommel of his sword, and he nearly loses consciousness.

"Tighten the cord," orders the evil old man.

The little man twists the cord using a small rod attached to its two joined ends, like a garrote. The coarse hemp bites into my flesh, crushes my fingers. It feels as if my joints will be dislocated. But I can overcome this pain. I say nothing.

"Tighter."

Again the cord is twisted. The thought crosses my mind that if they tighten it one more time, I'll never be able to use my fingers again.

"Tighter."

The flesh bursts open in places, blood oozes out on the bruised skin and runs down to my wrists. I close my eyes against the pain but can't hold back a long moan.

"One last time, did he rape you, yes or no?"

I still don't say a word. Oh my God, my hands, my precious hands, but still, I would sooner lose them, give up painting, rather than condemn Agostino with my own confession.

"Tighten the cord!"

Taking a deep breath, I can already hear the ghastly sound my bones will make in being crushed.

"Stop!" Agostino cries out, "Stop!"

"We will not stop until we have heard the whole truth."

Breaking free from the guards who had been hard pressed to hold him back, my adventurer throws himself on the torturer and pushes him away. "I raped her," he says. "Torture me if you will, but leave her in peace. I raped Artemisia who was a virgin. I took her by force, the first time, then I repeatedly took her afterward, promising her marriage. Punish me! She has done nothing to merit suffering like this. I am to blame for everything!"

He caresses the ends of my swollen fingers and contemplates in horror and guilt the blood that is still trickling down my arms. A tear runs down his cheek.

"That's better! Untie the girl," orders the judge. "As for him, he'll await his sentence in prison."

39

I was tossing in bed for long days, vacillating between complete delirium and a state of semiconsciousness, racked with a fever that seemed as though it should certainly kill me, while doctors and healers crowded around my bedside—some diagnosing a sickness of the body, due to an infection in the blood; others a sickness of the brain, due to the corruption of my soul—and my father, sick with worry, prayed to God, had novenas executed for my recovery, and dozens of candles burned. Agostino, my poor, sweet love, was declared guilty of rape and sentenced to two years in prison.

Orazio was outraged. "Two years? That's nothing! He deserves penal servitude! Death!"

He would have liked for the Roman system of justice to be more severe. As for the judge, he found that the plaintiffs should consider themselves lucky that the court had not decided to prosecute them, the father for his repeated lies and the daughter for her impious drawings.

The guards came to take Agostino to the cell whose four walls would be his sole horizon for the coming years. As he was being led away, my adventurer had called out to the man who sired me, "We've both lost her, Orazio. You certainly haven't obtained a very high price for your daughter, and I will always regret her. We've both acted like a couple of egotistical fools. But my eyes were dazzled with love, whereas you were blinded by hate and vanity."

❦

When the desire to live finally triumphed over the will to die, the fever released its hold. It had left me weakened, but more clearer minded and more determined than before the sickness. While I was convalescing, Nicolo, my father's agent, came to visit me. The first sentence he pronounced immediately revealed his designs.

"I spoke with the doctor," he informed me. "He assures me you will soon regain the use of your fingers."

The words were not dictated by simple compassionate concern on his part. He was speaking as a professional worried about the physical capacities of his young colt. With Nicolo, self-interest always came first.

"The grand duke was very impressed with your *Lucretia*," he went on, "and moved by the tribulations you have been going through. Desirous to make your life more pleasant, to ensure your future, and to firmly establish your reputation, His Excellency invites you to take up residence in his court. Apartments have already been reserved for you in his palace in Florence."

I turned my face away, but I couldn't help thinking excitedly, *Florence, the mother of all art, the city of Giotto, the father of modern painters, Florence, the native land of the pious Fra Angelico, the inventive Masaccio, the enchanting Botticelli, the divine Leonardo da Vinci, the powerful Michelangelo, Florence . . . soon to be the land of Artemisia Gentileschi's exile.* Although I was aware of the injustice of the situation—Agostino was in prison while I was free and, according to Nicolo, looking forward to a promising future—I couldn't help but quiver with pleasure at the idea of being taken into the pantheon of artists, the city in which masterpieces are to be found on every street corner, in every church, and each chapel. I could already see myself visiting San Lorenzo, Santa Maria del Carmine, the Boboli gardens and the classical collection there, Santa Maria del Fiore, whose dome, constructed by Brunelleschi, is still admired by the entire world. How I would have loved to visit the marvels that Agostino grew up with in his company. And I will! By love's magic, the two of us will walk hand in hand, through the wonders of Florence. My adventurer is a part of me from now on. No matter where

I go, he will always be with me. Although this is a great consolation to me, is it really for him? Can the fact that I carry him in my heart like a beautiful wounded bird, incapable of flying on its own, be enough for him?

So despite a few pangs of guilt, I accepted the grand duke's invitation with unbridled joy. No sooner had Nicolo disappeared, than I jumped from my bed, hastily filled two trunks with my personal effects, clothing and art materials, and had my tent studio taken down. There was another reason for wanting to leave the house as quickly as possible: I had come to despise my father's company.

Orazio was surprised, disoriented. He tried to prevent me from leaving. He clung to me, pleading, speaking of the work we still had to accomplish together, the wonderful plans we had made, the eternal partnership that he had dreamed up the day I had been refused at the Academy. I stared straight at the man who had been the cause of all of my misfortunes, the father and mentor I had once loved so much. In a harsh and already distant voice, I said, "Do you expect me to finish your frescoes, or paint over Agostino's?"

Seeing my father so unhappy didn't make me soften until it was time to say good-bye. "Don't worry about me. You have given me something that no one can ever take away and for which I will be forever grateful. You taught me how to paint and also that life itself should be as intense as a painting."

Orazio shook his head. "I gave you the pain that you put into your work, not your talent."

I took his hands, already mottled with age, in my still bandaged fingers. "You made things easier for me by barring the routes that could have made me turn away from art," I answered. "If I had remained a respectable woman, I would have undoubtedly ended up getting married, abandoning my paintbrushes to devote myself to a household and children. Now I am no longer even a woman, my only love from now on will be painting."

I had promised myself that I would remain faithful to Agostino, yet had resolved never to attempt, by any means, to see him again—a happy couple can't be founded upon smoldering ruins. I swore to myself that, after him, no other man would ever be permitted to share my bed again. I had decided to devote myself to God, the supreme force that I would laud in my canvases and with my colors, taking the vows in my own way, not with a cornet or a rosary, but with a paintbrush in hand.

The horse-drawn cart was waiting in front of the white fence that could barely be distinguished in the pale morning mists. Fulvio, my lifelong friend, had come to say good-bye. I made a present of my self-portrait to him. "I'll hang it in our cave, Artemisia. That way, I won't feel so alone. I can talk to you, and you'll hear me, even if you won't be able to answer." Handing me a beautiful string of fish, whittled naïvely out of wood and colorfully painted, he said, "Here, just as I promised, jewels from the sea!"

I put the curious necklace he had made around my neck and hugged Fulvio very tightly. My fisherman friend turned and ran quickly away without looking back. Then I went into my father's studio, where I found young Vito lying on his pallet, asleep, his dirty cheeks smudged with tears. He had flopped down there, exhausted and inconsolable, and taken comfort in sleep. I picked the child up in my arms, carried him to the cart, and lay him down on some blankets. He opened one eye and a wide smile spread across his face.

"Of course I'm taking you with me," I said to him, "whatever would become of me without you?" He pretended to flex his muscles to show me how strong he was, and flung his arms around my neck, laughing.

Standing next to Tuzia, my little brother Marco was desperately observing the scene. "And me?"

I knelt down in front of him and kissed him over and over again on his hair, on his cute little nose, his lips, his forehead. "I can't take you with me, my little love, but I won't forget you. Florence isn't that far away, you know, you can come and see me often." I slipped his small fist into Tuzia's strong hand. "You never knew your real mama, Marco. Tuzia is a mother to you, and that is the most precious thing in the world."

I could have sworn that Tuzia shot a touched and grateful look at me. As I was walking away she held me back. "Don't go away, Artemisia. If you go, your father will surely die."

"No," I answered, shaking my head. "You know I must go, and he knows it too. But you can rest easy, one does not die of a broken heart, that is something I have learned."

And that is how I left my father's house forever.

EPILOGUE

Today, sailing under the English flag on the galleon that is taking me back to Italy, now that torpid reminiscences have given way to present reality, the ashen-haired woman I have now become is lost in sober thought. I feel as though I've come full circle in reconciling myself with my father and, despite the little time I have left to live, am thereby all the more at peace with myself and free to begin a new life. If that be the case, how can the years of my adolescence—from the moment I left the convent until my exile in Florence began—be evaluated? Is it actually necessary to evaluate them? The hopes and the disappointments, can it all be tallied up in two columns just like in an accountant's ledger? In a way, it is enough for me to have unraveled the tangled threads of that era, which, in its very confusion, was so decisive for me, and to have fully recognized the enormous influence that all of the events that took place back then had upon me. So much so that it was stamped automatically on my personality, for all to see, just like the wrinkles that line my face. Whatever path we decide to take defines who we are, it shapes us as we move gradually down it, until it is the path alone that counts—there is nothing to be attained at the end. All attempts at evaluation would be vain.

My pious resolutions, the mute promise I had made to Agostino to devote myself to God, to live only for the Supreme Being, lauding Him through my paintbrush—I'm no longer angry with myself for not having kept them. I continued to paint, that's the most important thing, and I will continue to paint until the day I die. That's what will tip the scales on the day of judgment. Of course, my conception of art was somewhat modified by practical considerations. Life wasn't always easy, and I was alone, had no man to support me, bringing up as best I could my adopted son, Vito, who has grown to be a handsome man and an accomplished painter. I helped to set him up in his own studio. He's my pride and joy. We're almost the same age and the incorrigible jester still delights in calling me Mama!

But the idealism that had prompted me, as a young girl, to vow that I would never stoop to groveling, was stifled by frequenting the corrupt courts in which I practiced my craft, and by the whims of my clients, prelates, and princes. Like all artists, even those that I previously held in contempt for the way in which they bowed and scraped, I ended up compromising, matching, if need be, the colors of my paintings with those of the rooms where they would be hung, substituting, at the very last minute, the magnificent face of an ancient heroine with the features of the wife or the mistress of my patron whenever the fancy took him. I also did quite a few portraits, thereby following Tuzia's advice. One isn't required to pay the model—instead it is the model who pays! In other words, I quickly grew to be exactly like everyone else, and I was successful at it; I have never been in want of work, and I have always brought as much respect to the name of Gentileschi as my father did. What do youthful dreams matter at my age? If I had remained as impetuous and stubborn as I was at sixteen, what would have become of me? Perhaps I would be a hermit working in some a remote cave, a disheveled and insane woman, painting absurd images for her own pleasure, thrusting her clawlike finger into the entrails of animals to give body to her deranged visions with their blood. I probably wouldn't have been a far cry from that. Being a woman and a painter is a heavy enough load to carry without also having to bear the burden of an irascible disposition. How far away and fragile the young Artemisia seems now, she who so passionately idealized everything around her! Yet I don't believe I have become bitter; at least I am not any longer. I simply have a few scratches to show from life's thorns. The way in which I used to sublimate everything, gesticulate, storm around at times to make myself heard, strikes me today as terrribly naive, if not downright indecent. I have learned to express my emotions with lines, and it has helped me to become more profound and more tolerant as well: the two often do go hand in hand. What other way of letting out my feelings could serve me as well as my art. I've grown to be almost silent with time, very reserved, yet I'm able to make myself understood much more easily. I use the circuitous means of the paintbrush, communicating my thoughts through images, investing my figures with my own sensitivity, and thereby laying it bare for all the world to see.

Suddenly, it occurs to me how absurd it is for me to be questioning myself in this way at over fifty years of age. It is the young Artemisia who is again demanding that old accounts be settled! Her again! She certainly hasn't lost any of her desire for vindication! What can I say to her? I have argued many times over that I am now at peace with myself, that I feel as though I've lived a full and meaningful life, the little pest still isn't satisfied.

Not satisfied? Yes, as a matter of fact I am, at least as far as the overall picture goes, especially since I made up with Orazio. Now, I see my past in a completely different light. As long as he and I were not on good terms, I had the exasperating feeling of having left an unfinished painting behind me, and guilt weighed heavy on my shoulders.

The ambiguous relationship with my father, so tumultuous and intense, initially founded upon exclusiveness, and later destroyed by jealousy, was in a way my first love affair, with all the disillusions and indellible sorrows that this implies. It undoubtedly affected all the relationships I had with men afterward. The stage had been set. With Agostino, the very first, the mad dreams had all ended in rack and ruin. Incapable of seeing them through, I somehow undermined each of my love affairs without really intending to. The only time that I did build something with a man, for I did end up getting married, I managed to find a father for my daughter, Ada, my most beautiful accomplishment, who was so completely devoid of redeeming qualities that it was unthinkable not to rid myself of him as quickly as possible. I have no idea where my husband, whose very face I have forgotten, is today. He gave me a child who is unique, magnificent, and that is all I asked of him. When the day came to dower my cherished daughter, relinquishing my last scruples, I barraged my patrons with a torrent of letters, imploring them to help me, begging ten ecus here, fifty florins there, weeping, unabashedly confessing my financial woes. It wasn't that they were so terribly serious—I make a substantial living—but that is simply the custom in a sphere in which it is virtually impossible for a painter to get paid. The game between clients and artists consists in, for the former, interminably putting off their debts, and for the latter, humbly begging on bended knees. Did not Bramante and Leonardo da Vinci spend much of their time pleading misery? That is how our Maecenases set the balance straight—we have the talent, whereas they have the money and the desire to acquire works of art. They like to make it perfectly clear to us that without them, our very existence would be meaningless.

As I was unable to build a significant bond with a man, I got into the habit of choosing my lovers from among the young men of noble birth. They offer many advantages. Still wrapped in the fragile grace of adolescence, they are very well mannered, do not lack in interesting conversation, which is always pleasant, and above all, since a wonderful marriage arrangement awaits them elsewhere, they don't need to latch on to me.

"You should have remained faithful to Agostino, you swore that you would!" young Artemisia fumes in my ear. How can I answer her? I lived every minute of the time that my lover was in prison in symbiosis with his memory, visiting in his invisible company, as I had planned, all the churches in Florence, talking to him aloud, not caring whether people thought I was insane, answering with poise that I was already spoken for, to all those who courted me. Informed as to the date of his release, and in spite of the decision I had made to never see him again, I hurried off to Rome. I couldn't wait to throw myself into his arms, to tell him that everything was behind us, that I loved him as though nothing had ever happened to damage our love. The jailer, the same one who had let me into Agostino's cell two years earlier, told me that he had left the city. I didn't understand, he couldn't have been unaware that I was coming, I had sent word! It was impossible that he didn't love me, the jailer showed me the many portraits he had done of me, from memory, during his incarceration, and that he had left behind.

"The prisoner said that the paintings were for you. If my memory is correct, he also said that they were a testimony of his love. Quite a strange fellow, he was! . . . No, I don't know where he went. He took a boat to Spain, I think, or maybe it was France."

Several years passed and I still heard nothing concerning Tassi. In the end, I stopped searching for him, I became introverted, began to work relentlessly, satisfying myself with the imagined love of the great wounded bird that I carried in my heart and whose name was Agostino.

One evening, in the season that lovers celebrate, I saw my handsome adventurer again. It was surprisingly cold for the month of April, the flowers were late in blooming, and not a sparrow was to be heard. He had set himself up in a studio on the outskirts of Naples that one of his old students by the name of Claude Gellée, often called Claude Lorrain, had let him use. He was attempting, without much conviction, to find buyers for his already old-fashioned sea and landscapes. It was rumored that the only thing that really interested him now was astronomy. I had learned about all of his setbacks in minute detail. A hundred mouths busily kept me informed as soon as his return to Italy was made known.

"A solid couple can't be founded upon smoldering ruins," said a small voice that I was striving to keep quiet. Agostino was the love of my life and I would have done anything to get him back! At one of the windows, I gave three rapid knocks, followed by three slow ones—our old code—and walked in. Agostino was standing very stiffly in the center of the single room, fiddling awkwardly with the hem of his doublet. It was clear that he regretted having risen from his chair before I even walked in, that he was feeling a little idiotic, standing there at attention like that. My own embarrassment stemmed from his. Although Agostino had put on a little flesh, he hadn't lost much of his commanding beauty. In spite of the obvious uneasiness, his eyes sparkled, and a profusion of gallant phrases spilled from his lips, as if the trial, his prison term, and exile had rolled off of him without leaving a trace. His attitude was so incongruous that I couldn't find much to say to him and felt ill at ease with the man who was, in the end, such a far cry from what I had always imagined. The beautiful wounded bird that I carried in my heart, that I had nourished for so long with the seeds of my passion, now only vaguely resembled the person that was standing before me. Had it really been inevitable that my fate be tied to this man? We separated, feeling terribly embarrassed, promising to see each other again soon.

I left Agostino's house filled with bitterness and disappointment, yet at the same time, I was happy to have seen him again. Happy because I had found him so much shallower than in my memories, glad to be free of him at last, to open the cage and watch the great wounded bird fly away.

With time, even bad memories end up turning into happy ones. I never saw Agostino again, but today, standing on the deck of this ship with the sea spray lashing at my worn face, I see things differently. A cool, healing wave flows over my heart, then ebbs, leaving the soft sands of real emotions bare. Gratitude grips my entire being as if, in an infinite sigh, I have just now understood Agostino's ultimate sacrifice, the magnificent feat of love that he accomplished for me—first of all in vanishing from my life, and then later when I finally succeeded in my stubborn quest to see him again, in appearing to be as unattractive as possible. He had done it purposefully, I understand now. He who had known physical imprisonment wished to liberate me from the chains he had put around my heart. He gave me my freedom back.

Young Artemisia, now I can finally look you straight in the eye, my ledgers have been tallied: being a woman in a man's world, I did the very best I could.